The Christmas Spirit

Also by Susan Buchanan

Sign of the Times
The Dating Game
Return of the Christmas Spirit
Just One Day - Winter

The Christmas Spirit

SUSAN BUCHANAN

First published in 2013 by Susan Buchanan

A CIP catalogue record of this title is available from the British Library
Paperback – 978-0-9931851-8-2
eBook – 978-0-9931851-2-0

DEDICATION

For baby Antonia
On your first Christmas
Lots of love, Mummy xxx

ABOUT THE AUTHOR

Susan Buchanan lives in Scotland with her husband, their two young children and a crazy Labrador called Benji. She has been reading since the age of four and had to get an adult library card early as she had read the entire children's section by the age of ten. As a freelance book editor, she has books for breakfast, lunch and dinner and in her personal reading always has several books on the go at any one time.

If she's not reading, editing or writing, she's thinking about it. She loves romantic fiction, psychological thrillers, crime fiction and legal thrillers, but her favourite books feature books themselves.

In her past life she worked in International Sales as she speaks five languages. She has travelled to 51 countries and her travel knowledge tends to pop up in her writing. Collecting books on her travels, even in languages she doesn't speak, became a bit of a hobby.

Susan writes contemporary fiction, partly set in Scotland, usually featuring travel, food or Christmas. When not working, writing, or caring for her two delightful cherubs, Susan loves reading (obviously), the theatre, quiz shows and eating out – not necessarily in that order!

You can connect with Susan via her website www.susanbuchananauthor.com or on Facebook www.facebook.com/susan.buchanan.author and on Twitter @susan_buchanan or Instagram authorSusanBuchanan

ACKNOWLEDGEMENTS

Huge thanks to
Jaboof Design Studio for my gorgeous cover. What
a decision that was to make – too many gorgeous
possibilities to choose from! –
Claire@jaboofdesignstudio.com

Tracie, Sam, the Chicklit Goddesses, Judee, Laura,
Tony for putting up with my seriously unsociable hours
and mood swings, and last but not least my Twitter and
Facebook followers and all the book bloggers who help
spread the word.

Chapter One

D-Day!

Well, my D-Day anyway, thought Natalie.

Every year on this day, the first of December, her raison d'être and her job, as such, began. It only lasted a month, but her personal deadline was always twenty-four days. The other week was just to ensure there was no unfinished business.

Natalie hoped this Christmas would be a good one for everyone. If she had anything to do with it, as in the past, those she chose would have a Christmas to remember.

This year she would be working in the small town of Winstanton about twenty miles north of Glasgow; more of a village really, with its carefully tended lawns, idyllic cottages and splendid views over Loch Lomond.

Each year Natalie had to choose a different country. This was her first visit to Scotland. She hoped she would get used to the Scottish accent and that her own would go unnoticed. Speaking several languages came in handy, but it was even better to blend in like a local.

Although Natalie's job actively only lasted one month per year, her preparation lasted ten months. Well, she did get some holidays. Ten months in which to research, narrow down and shortlist her candidates. It was no easy task, as although a small town, Winstanton still had fifteen thousand residents and Natalie could only choose four. Now, she couldn't possibly check them all out, could she? No. Natalie had a gift which helped her. She could feel other people's happiness. The downside was, she could also feel their unhappiness. Marvellous, eh?

Natalie readjusted her handbag on her shoulder and grabbed hold of the handle of her carry-on case, dragging it along the deserted platform of Winstanton train station. She had picked up the keys to her new one-bedroom cottage earlier that day in Glasgow. Now all she had to do was make her way there. There wasn't a taxi in sight; not surprising, since she was the only person who had got off at the station. Fortunately there was a phone box, an old-style red one – how quaint. Even luckier, it hadn't been vandalised and it had a Yellow Pages in it which hadn't been ripped to shreds. Natalie had never got around to getting a mobile phone. There was no reception where she lived most of the year, so there seemed little point. Taking out a piece of paper from her purse, she dialled the first taxi number she'd come across in her research of the area; she was nothing if not prepared. In her job she had to be. She was looking forward to her new role. Her job was always a job within a job; a little difficult to explain, but it was kind of like a secondment.

The taxi arrived soon after. Natalie could imagine there wasn't much doing for a taxi driver on a Sunday night. A cheery old man, probably in his sixties, greeted her. 'Miss Hope?'

'The very same.'

'Let me help you with your case.'

'Thanks,' said Natalie, when he swung it with some

effort into the boot.

'What have you got in there, bricks?'

Natalie laughed and said, 'Wouldn't you like to know.'

He looked as if he would indeed like to know, but was too polite to push it further.

They arrived at Rose Cottage within ten minutes.

'Five pounds eighty, hen.'

'Worth every penny,' Natalie said. She handed him seven pounds and told him to keep the change.

'Do you want me to wait until you see if anyone's home?' asked the driver, eyeing the darkened cottage.

'No, it's OK, thanks, although that's kind of you to be so thoughtful. I have a key.'

'No problem. Have a nice night.'

'You too. Hope it's a busy one for you.'

The driver's expression conveyed that was unlikely to be the case.

She noticed he didn't leave until she was safely inside the cottage and she'd switched on the hall light. Nice soul, obviously a happy man. He wouldn't be needing her help.

Natalie closed the door behind her and surveyed her new living quarters. The darkness had made it difficult to notice much about the garden outside, and the driving rain had made her keen to get inside as quickly as possible. She found herself in a small hallway, with a deep pile carpet, mocha in colour. She couldn't wait to slip off her boots and luxuriate in the feel of the pile between her toes. Her feet ached from the journey; it was rather a long way.

An antique mirror hung from a hook in the hallway, which was dimly lit by a fake gas lamp. Off the hall were five doors. The first turned out to be a cupboard, also home to the boiler. The second led her into a country kitchen, complete with French dresser and pine table and chairs, with an Aga taking centre stage; the kitchen was well-equipped and quite spacious, considering it was a one-bedroom cottage. Natalie exited the kitchen and tried the next door – her bedroom for the next month. A double bed, a large wardrobe and two bedside cabinets made up the room, nothing special, but comfortable enough. On the other side of the hall, the first door she tried led into the bathroom.

Oh, what a treat! A tiled wet room.

For a cottage, it was modern; a rare mix of old meets new.

The last door led her into a large living room with a bay window overlooking the front garden. She hadn't been aware of how far up the hill the driver had come, but now she could see, even in the dark, the splendid views over Loch Lomond. Lights twinkled in the distance; she assumed they were from moored boats, or a boathouse perhaps.

The living room welcomed her with a coal fire. Lovely. It required extra effort, but would definitely be worth it. Natalie planned on cosy nights in after work, although she did expect to be working long hours, relaxing in front of the fire with a good book, or cooking on the Aga. Bliss. The corner sofa wasn't to her taste, but was new and clearly from the period when corner sofas were back in fashion. Heavy curtains hung over the bay window, keeping out the cold.

Yes, this'll do nicely.

She returned to the kitchen and opened the fridge. Aw, the lady who had leased her the house and the bakery had included a few goodies for her first night. How sweet, and much appreciated, since Natalie was worn out from the journey. She checked out the cupboards to see about pots and pans. Two bottles of red wine greeted her when she opened the first door and she made a mental note to thank the landlady; just what she needed to go with her first meal and help her unpack. Tomorrow would be a long day and a new start.

Chapter Two

Midday. Not that time meant anything much to him any more. Midday was much the same as one o'clock, which was similar to three o'clock or five o'clock, for that matter. Stanley didn't have big events in his day – the most he had were his three meals, and even those weren't exciting. He simply didn't have the stomach for them any more. In fact, he had little interest in anything any more; not since his Edith passed away back in July.

They'd been married sixty-five years; childhood sweethearts. She'd waited for him during the war. Many hadn't. He knew lots of fellows who had returned from the war to discover their sweetheart had taken up with some other man in their absence. Some got fed up waiting, others were misinformed that their beloved had perished. There had been such confusion during the war, both for the troops and the civilians. It had been difficult to keep abreast of such matters. But not his Edith; his Edie. After the end of the war, as soon as it was decent, they had married. He had always known he wanted to marry Edie, from the moment they were introduced at a friend's party.

Stanley poured himself a cup of tea, Typhoo, Edie's favourite brand, and then poured a cup for Edie. He knew

6

she wasn't sitting opposite him in body, but she was there in spirit and in his memories. Some would call him a daft old codger, but it comforted him. He didn't go so far as to make her meals, though. That would just be plain crazy, but a cup of tea was one of the traditions they had enjoyed most together. Everything could be fixed with a cup of tea. Well, almost anything. The cancer had taken his beautiful Edie, on the twenty-eighth of July, a Sunday. She had battled it for five years on and off, thought she'd beaten it, but in the end it had still claimed her. A tear came to his eye as he remembered how brave she had been in the face of the disease that had wracked her small body. Far braver than him. Here was he, alone and unable to cope with the little things he needed to do on a day-to-day basis. Edie had done so much for him. He had always appreciated her, but never more than once she had gone. His angel. Today was the second of December and he was glad to see the last month of the year arrive; he couldn't wait for this year to be over, for all it signified. But he was dreading Christmas. Edie had loved Christmas. How could he have one without her? How could he bear it? It didn't even warrant thinking about. He felt too desolate to have Christmas. As far as he was concerned, Christmas was cancelled. Edie would be cross with him, he knew, but some things couldn't be surmounted. He couldn't act full of the joys of spring, or in this case, Christmas, if he didn't feel it. And he needed Edie by his side to feel it. With a sigh, he picked up his newspaper and made a futile attempt at reading. Everything was such an effort these days.

Chapter Three

Meredith Storm finished signing the papers her PA had placed in front of her and barked, 'Anything else?'

Sophie shook her head and retreated.

Meredith didn't *see* Sophie, nor did she acknowledge all of the extra tasks Sophie completed for her at a moment's notice. Sophie was a cog in the wheel. She did what was asked of her. That was her role, as far as Meredith was concerned. She would never ask of anyone something she wouldn't be prepared to do herself. That left little, as Meredith was a workaholic. She never took days off, had to be forced almost at gunpoint to go on holiday, never called in sick, nor had time off for dental or hospital appointments. She was a machine. She started at six in the morning and finished at eleven at night, five days a week. On the weekends she went easy on herself, working from home for a great part of the two days.

She saw nothing wrong with calling Sophie up on a Saturday night and asking her to run off a report on the percentage increase and/or decrease of monthly sales over the past year in Ghana and have it across to her within half an hour. She wasn't like the rest of us. Sleep was an alien concept to her; she could often be found in the park at five o'clock in the morning doing yoga, or depending on her mood or her need for adrenalin, running or cycling through Loch Lomond and the Trossachs National Park. Her food shopping was delivered – one of those 'fresh food to the door' mob. She didn't cook, but she did eat out at the weekends, or ordered in to the office when she worked late. But a lifetime of takeaways, albeit healthy ones, hadn't given Meredith a lardy physique. *Au contraire*, she had the silhouette of a catwalk model. She couldn't care less; she wasn't out to impress anyone. She used men as and when she needed them, and women could bitch all they liked about her; it made no difference. Ambition was her drug of choice and she thrived on achievement.

CEO of her own telecommunications company at the age of twenty-five, Meredith made sure everyone knew about it. She delegated when essential, but she didn't really trust anyone to do as good a job as she could do herself. Her staff tolerated her, all twenty-nine of them. She had a fear of flying which she wouldn't admit to anyone, and had undergone hypnotherapy as well as other measures to get her on a plane. She still needed to pop a few pills, now and then, before boarding. She was the epitome of a workaholic and never let anyone get close. She had been married once and that had been her at her lowest ebb. Never again would she let someone get inside her head like that. Theo had broken her heart, typical Frenchman; lying, cheating scumbag. Didn't she know it was OK for Frenchmen to have mistresses? he'd asked her. Of course, her being English, how could she understand? he had said.

She hadn't known there was anything wrong. They had a fantastic sex life, they got on well, they shared many interests. Theo would buy her flowers, jewellery, sexy lingerie. Outwardly he gave the impression of a man in love. Why would he stray? Sure she worked a lot, but so did he, as sales director at a leading food retailer. Had he felt emasculated by her and her success? Now, at forty, she didn't care what anyone thought. She had never let anyone else *in* and had a preference for men who couldn't get too attached to her. Married men were perfect as a distraction, usually eager to indulge in clandestine sexual encounters, no strings attached. Perfect. And they left her alone on the big occasions. Christmas topped the list, Valentine's Day – the Hallmark holiday as she had nicknamed it – what a waste of time, and their birthdays; it saved her splurging on them.

Although generous with her money, Meredith couldn't understand the concept of generosity of time. Her family were forever inviting her to social occasions; she had a large extended family who met often at her parents' sprawling house in the country. Meredith rarely attended, preferring instead to pore over spreadsheets, participate in conference calls with Japan and Brazil, and keep an eye on the competition. Christmas was just one such occasion where she neglected her family. This year, twenty-one of them would gather at her sister Amelia's house, filling it until it almost burst at the seams. They would be pouring out of the kitchen, the dining room, and the living room, and the kids would probably take over the bedrooms to play the latest computer games. She knew this only because she had been told it all before. She'd only been once. The rest of the time she spent Christmas at her house, watching whatever American crime drama she was into that year on box set, sipping Pinot Noir and preparing a Waitrose meal for herself.

It would be safe to say she wasn't a Christmas person. No tree, no decorations, no turkey, no carols, no Queen's

Speech. The only Christmas-related tradition she respected was giving presents. She prided herself on choosing great gifts. She enjoyed picking out presents, although she did most of it online these days. She garnered snippets from her family on the few occasions when she saw or spoke to them, about other family members' interests, and she always managed to select the perfect gift. She had a knack for wrapping them and always gave an elaborately decorated box, with bows, stars and flowers stuck to it, so out of character with everyone's opinion of her: hard and stern. She was a contradiction all right, an enigma.

Chapter Four

Jacob hated signing on. It was so degrading. Even as a twenty-two-year-old, he could feel the shame. He knew that for people in their fifties who had worked all their days, then found themselves out of work due to this damned recession, it galled them to have to ask for help from the state. But they needed to, and so did he. It wasn't much, but it helped.

No matter how many interviews he was invited to, and there weren't that many in comparison with how many applications he had made, he had never been offered a job. Four years of university and no job. He had struggled through university, working in bars and even as a bingo caller at one point, but he couldn't even find that kind of work now. And for what, he had a 2:1 degree in Politics and Sociology. What use was it to him? He couldn't even get a second interview at a call centre. What kind of failure did that make him? He was well-turned-out, had a nice manner and he thought he was relatively charming, yet the job offers were unforthcoming. To top it all, there was the not so small matter of twenty thousand pounds of student loans to pay back in the future.

Jacob's family were rich, not just well off, but properly

stinking rich. You would think that would mean money wouldn't worry him, but his parents were of the belief that you had to earn everything in life. So, no, they hadn't bankrolled him through university. When he'd asked for help, they'd reminded him that they'd parted with enough money in the years when he had attended Gordonstoun. If they told him one more time that not everyone was lucky enough to go to the famous school attended by Prince Charles and Prince Philip, he'd do them a serious injury. So, Jacob had found himself jobs whilst at university and paid his own way. Why he ever thought his family would help him, was beyond him. Hadn't they shipped him off to Scotland at the first possible opportunity? His parents lived in rural Bedfordshire, with apartments in London, Hong Kong, New York and Dublin, as well as condos in North Carolina and Santa Monica. His father had worked for the diplomatic service and his mother, although a trained lawyer, had chosen to travel around the world with her husband, doing some freelance work when she got bored, but mainly playing the part of diplomat's wife, hosting dinner parties and attending tennis club events. A pity, then, that they didn't see fit to include their son in their plans.

In the beginning Jacob had loathed boarding school. He hated being away from home, but over time he had felt more at home at Gordonstoun and when on holiday at his friends' houses than he did in his own house. When he had then gone on to study at the University of Glasgow, some of those alliances had been broken, or perhaps not upheld as well as they had all expected. Life sent them in different directions. Many of his peers had parents who employed them in their firms; some owned their own companies at the forefront of technology, were inventors or had made canny investment choices long ago. Others came from old money, so had no need to work, enabling them to pick and choose their role.

Jacob was an exception. His father could have put a word in for him at the civil service, although Jacob wasn't sure he was cut out for officialdom, it was too stuffy for him, but he didn't. Jacob was to carve his own path and his own luck. His father had worked for everything all his life and he expected his son to do the same. Nothing would be handed to him on a plate. Jacob didn't expect that. He wanted to make his own mark. What he hadn't foreseen was his father's coldness, or rather indifference. He had presumed he would review his decision not to help him get ahead, due to the current difficulties in finding a job, as a result of the recession. Surely it was better for him to have a job, than for his father to be embarrassed by his son being on the dole? Being jobless was another reason Jacob didn't keep in touch with many of his fellow alumni. He was ashamed. He knew it wasn't his fault. He was doing everything humanly possible to get a job, but he simply wasn't having any luck. Even working for free hadn't earned him a job. Employers had just taken the free time he'd given them and when he'd enquired about some paid work, even if temporary, he had been met with a resounding *no*. It was seriously demoralising.

At least he had his flat. His parents paid for that, an investment of course, Jacob thought bitterly. His father probably wrote it off against tax. He was so sick of having no money, not being able to go out with the friends he had who lived in the area, not having a girlfriend, as how would he take her out on a date with no cash? The utilities were paid, as well as the council tax and the flat itself, but apart from that, he was on his own. His father was a proponent of tough love. Sometimes Jacob wondered why his mother didn't intervene on his behalf, but then, his mother was weak. She followed his father blindly like a puppy. Maybe he didn't want to be in love after all, if it turned you into someone who asked no questions.

Jacob felt his failure to gain employment all the more keenly as his sister, Tabitha, ran her own digital communications agency. Only two years older than him, she was very successful. She had excelled at St George's School for Girls in Edinburgh and gone on to set up her own company. It would have been handy if she could have gone to St Margaret's in Aberdeen, to be close to her brother, but they didn't accept boarders. Likewise the top-rated school, for that's where their father wanted to send her, Wellington School in Ayr, accepted only day pupils; not a possibility when your father was a diplomat in Qatar. Again, Jacob wondered for the nth time why his parents had bothered having children at all. He and Tabitha had been reared by nannies since they were babies. His parents had never had time to care for them.

Until they reached secondary school age they had travelled to wherever their father was posted. Jacob's formative years had seen him at English schools in Hong Kong, Yemen, Peru and Zimbabwe. He had enjoyed his education, in more than one sense of the word. He had experienced so much and was a better person for having lived the life he had, but when he was eleven he had been sent to Gordonstoun and saw his parents only a few times a year; hard for a young boy about to go through puberty. Initially he had been scared, then apprehensive, and finally accepting. Since he had gone to boarding school he had only spent Christmas with his parents twice. The Caribbean or the Indian Ocean had always held more appeal for them at that time of year, and a teenage boy or girl would only get in the way. The few times per year he did see his parents were invariably when they were in the UK for business and took it upon themselves to visit their children. *How noble of them.* Jacob vowed either never to have children, or if his partner (should he be lucky enough ever to have one, and present times weren't indicative of a positive outcome in that respect) absolutely wanted them, then he would be the best father there had ever been. There would be no boarding school for his children.

'*Mr Carruthers?*'

Glancing up, Jacob saw a middle-aged, balding man with his tie askew and his sleeves rolled up, checking to see if he was in the waiting area. Jacob made his way over to the desk to sign on.

Chapter Five

Next morning dawned bright and clear, the previous night's rain dried up, so you would never have known it had been torrential less than twelve hours previously. Birds chirping in the trees outside her bedroom woke Natalie. She checked her watch and saw it was already nine o'clock. Goodness, she really had been tired. Well, she had better get up, as she had an awful lot to do. It was by sheer chance that the appointment she had with the bakery owner wasn't until eleven o'clock, so Natalie availed herself of the wet room, ate one of the delicious croissants her landlady had left for her and drank some coffee. She took her to-do list out of her bag and double-checked it. Yep, she thought she could get through all of that today, but first to open up shop.

Natalie stood and admired the shopfront before going in. The Sugar and Spice sign was made up of pink iced cakes, on a cream background, with a cherry on the top of the i of Spice. The writing sloped to the right as if italicised. Natalie had a good feeling about this year's secondment. She admired the sign one more time and then opened the door, causing the bell to jangle. Before her were a few mismatched wooden tables and chairs which lent the bakery a homely feel. She could imagine the townspeople enjoying a scone with clotted cream and a good pot of Scottish Breakfast or Earl Grey here. At the back of the shop stood the cash register and glass-fronted cases showcasing the day's wares. Natalie had barely time to glance round at the sugar pink décor and pictures adorning the walls of speciality cakes which the bakery had made in the past, before a woman entered from the back of the shop carrying a tray of pastries.

'Good morning, dear. Let me put these down and I'll be right with you.'

The woman laid the cakes on the counter and then turned to Natalie. 'Right, dear, what can I get you?'

'Are you Mrs Williams?'

'That's right, dear.'

'I'm Natalie Hope, Mrs Williams, pleased to meet you.' She extended her hand to the wizened old lady in front of her, who now untied her apron with a sense of finality.

'Lovely to meet you, dear. Welcome to Sugar and Spice. I'm sure you'll do a grand job.'

'Thanks, I'll try to keep it up to your high standards and not disappoint any of your regulars.'

'I don't think that will be a problem. You came highly recommended and have such a lot of experience. I'm honoured you want to work in my little bakery. I'm just surprised you don't have one or a chain of your own.'

'Oh, I'm between premises right now.'

'Ah,' said Mrs Williams, seemingly happy with that answer. 'Anyway, let me show you the ropes.'

Mrs Williams then spent a good half hour showing Natalie the ins and outs of the bakery: how to work the ovens, where the water turned off, the alarm system, as well as information on contacting the suppliers. She had no computer. Everything was written down by hand and archived in lever arch folders.

'So do you have any questions?' Mrs Williams asked, wringing her hands.

Natalie reassured Mrs Williams by telling her everything seemed straightforward, and invited her to stay and observe how she handled the customers for an hour or so, to give her peace of mind.

Mrs Williams was convinced by Natalie handing her a cup of tea and a scone with clotted cream.

Sugar and Spice didn't have the newfangled pieces of kit some other bakeries had, but Mrs Williams had something special which many of them didn't have – knowledge and years of experience. She knew what tasted good and what her customers wanted. For her part, she couldn't help but be a tad worried about handing over her business, albeit temporarily, to someone she barely knew, no matter how great their credentials. It was such a shame she had to go into hospital; pesky gall bladder. But she knew she'd already put it off enough, too long in fact. Now her recovery period would be longer. The doctor had said she should be OK to go back to work in January, if she behaved. *Six weeks rest*, he had said firmly. The operation was planned for nine o'clock the following morning.

First to arrive after Mrs Williams had seated herself at one of the few tables the bakery boasted was Mr Green, who worked at the post office opposite. As she sat there, she knew he would be in for his usual custard slice and a mug of coffee. She watched as Natalie greeted him warmly, prepared his coffee and popped his cake onto a plate, before telling him that would be two pounds ninety-five. Mr Green then took himself off to one of the unoccupied tables and sat down to read his newspaper. Engrossed in his reading, he didn't notice the flaky pastry landing on his jumper, as he bit into it. *Men*, thought Mrs Williams. *So messy*. But she was pleased. Mr Green always ate her cakes with such relish.

Miss Leather, a retired schoolteacher, was next to arrive. She said hello to Mrs Williams and introduced herself to Natalie. She'd heard all about her in the run-up to Mrs Williams' operation. She'd be fine, though. Nothing to worry about; just routine. Miss Leather ordered two chocolate éclairs for her and her elder sister, who lived with her now; 'Better than her being put in a nursing home,' she'd said. Poor dear didn't get out much, but how she enjoyed her chocolate éclairs. Oh, and a couple of empire biscuits for teatime.

Miss Leather was telling Mrs Williams how a friend of hers had recently had her gall bladder removed and was back to normal in a month, when Stanley arrived. Stanley had been coming to Sugar and Spice for two decades. Edie had loved their Eccles cake, whilst macaroon was Stanley's favourite. He didn't know what Mrs Williams put in it, but it was delicious, far superior to those shop-bought ones.

There was nothing physically wrong with Stanley; he just didn't see the point of doing much any more, without Edie. But even he had to venture out from time to time, and when he did, he liked to retain the habits he had shared with Edie when she was alive. A weekly visit to the bakery had been part of that ritual.

'Good morning, how are you today?' Natalie asked.

'Not bad, hen. How are you? New, are you? Taking over whilst Jessie's in hospital?' said Stanley, nodding hello to Mrs Williams, before extracting a handkerchief and blowing his nose. 'Sorry, hen, it's this weather. Thank goodness we're getting a break from it today.'

'Yes, it has been pretty cold and wet recently, hasn't it?

Nice to see a bit of sun for a change,' Natalie agreed. 'So what can I get you?'

'A macaroon, please.' Stanley inclined his head to the coconut-covered treat.

'Coming right up. So any plans for the day?'

Caught off guard, Stanley stammered, then surprised himself by saying, 'I might go for a walk in the park, since it's so nice.'

'Sounds lovely. That's exactly what I would do if I wasn't working today. Where's the park, then?'

'Oh,' Stanley said, thinking, unaccustomed to being asked much these days. Edie was forever asking him questions, sometimes more than he would have liked, but what he wouldn't give now to have her back, bombarding him with questions. 'If you turn left when you go out of here and walk along to the stone bridge, turn right and the park is in front of you.'

'Excellent. I'll check it out.'

'Where are you staying?' asked Stanley, enjoying passing on some information to this pleasant young woman. She would be a good stand-in for Jessie.

'I'm at Rose Cottage,' Natalie informed him, as she put his cake in a bag.

'Lovely place. Used to visit it as a boy. It belonged to my grandfather originally.'

'Oh, is that so? Well, you must tell me some stories about it sometime.'

'I'll do that, hen. I'll do that. Well, nice to meet you,' he said as Natalie put the exact money he had left on the counter in the till. 'I hope you enjoy working here.'

'I'm sure I will. Enjoy your walk.'

'Thanks,' said Stanley, then he left, the door chiming his departure.

Mrs Williams continued to watch Natalie's interaction with a few other customers. The hour was soon up and she told Natalie she was more than happy to leave her business in her capable hands.

'Why don't you stay to sample some of my cakes?' Natalie asked. 'I was just about to make a batch of empire biscuits. We're already running low. Is Tuesday empire biscuit day or something?'

'No, I don't know what it is today. I don't need to stick around, though, to taste your cakes, dear. I'm sure they'll be lovely. I'm just glad to see that you have the right personality to run the bakery. You have good manners and a nice way with the customers. You show an interest in them.'

'Well, I do love spending time with people. I find them fascinating. I love nothing better than sitting in a pavement café watching the world go by with a latte and a *pain au chocolat*.'

'Well, if that's all, dear, I think I'll head home, get some rest before tomorrow. I'm so sorry about leaving you in the lurch working alone, what with Nuala breaking her foot. The agency did say they would ensure they had someone to cover her by the end of the week.'

'Don't you worry about a thing. I'll be fine.'

The early part of the afternoon saw the café full of schoolchildren and young mothers who came in with their prams and buggies, picking up a treat either for themselves to devour before their other children got home, or for the children to have after dinner. Around two thirty, the door opened and a boy and a girl came in. The girl was well dressed, city chic, with a purple-and-pink scarf around her neck, effortlessly glam. The boy, by contrast, wore jeans which were hanging off him and Natalie didn't think he was trying to be fashionable. He could do with putting on a bit of weight.

'I can't believe you've never brought me here,' the girl said to her companion.

'I don't exactly have the cash for extras at the moment, sis,' the boy said, turning red.

'No problem, my treat. Did I tell you I signed another contract? UK-wide retailer, sixty stores, can't tell you the name yet. It's all under non-disclosure agreement,' she said whilst eyeing up the mouth-watering array of cakes.

Meanwhile the boy was scanning the busy café.

The girl turned around just then and said, 'Jacob, what would you like? I'm having some Rocky Road, caramel shortcake for later and chocolate fudge cake for tomorrow.' With that list, it would be easy to imagine that the girl was the size of a house but she, unfairly, resembled a rake.

Without turning around, the boy said, 'Fudge doughnut for me, Tabs, if they have them.'

It was soon ascertained that fudge doughnuts were available and the girl, Tabitha, paid for them.

As Tabitha turned to leave, Jacob addressed Natalie, who was behind the counter.

'Excuse me, I can't help noticing you're on your own. Are there any openings for staff, by any chance?'

Natalie smiled at him and said, 'I'm just filling in for the owner for a month, but we are a little short-staffed as her assistant has just broken her leg. I can't make any promises, but why don't I give her a call and see if she'd give you a trial? Do you have any experience?'

'Not in a bakery, but I've worked in pubs, if that helps, and I'm good with the public.'

'Let me see what I can do,' said Natalie as she lifted a tray of cakes out of the oven behind her.

'Would it be paid work?' Jacob squirmed at asking, but he was fed up working for nothing.

'I can't answer that, but I'll suggest that if you pass muster after a few hours, that she hire you and then you'd be paid.'

'That would be great. When will you know?'

'Why don't you come back tomorrow morning?' Natalie advised him.

'Thanks ever so much,' said Jacob, a smile breaking across his face.

It was clear to Natalie that it had cost him a lot to ask.

Tabitha had looked on bemused whilst this exchange took place. She beamed at her brother, and then mouthed *Thanks* to Natalie as they left the bakery.

Two down, two to go, Natalie thought.

There was no-one in the shop, so Natalie called Mrs Williams, apologised for bothering her, but explained about Jacob. Mrs Williams told her she must trust her judgement and they settled on an hourly rate, should Jacob prove to be up to the task. She stipulated that Natalie should obtain references for him, whether personal or work it didn't matter, but she wanted references to be sure he wasn't a serial killer and Natalie wasn't putting herself at risk by working alongside him. Natalie assured Mrs Williams she would take care of everything and hung up, silently hugging herself and chuckling at Mrs Williams' overactive imagination.

Chapter Six

How could Ethan do this to her? Rebecca didn't even bother trying to stem the tears. And what was all that rubbish about it being nothing she had done, they just wanted different things? She wanted the same things as him, didn't she? Three years wasted. Theirs was the first long-term relationship she'd been in, and now she had to sort through the rubble. He'd moved out until they could work out if they needed to sell the flat, or if she could afford to buy him out. He said no-one else was involved, but she didn't know if she believed him.

Men were rubbish at being on their own. Women took breakups far harder at the time, but got over them more easily in the long run. She had several male friends who had met someone else before breaking up with their current girlfriend, as they couldn't be without a girlfriend, or at least had to have a successor in mind. Rebecca began to question the late nights he had worked, the football matches he'd played at, but she'd later found his clean kit in the hall. When quizzed over it, Ethan had said he'd had a spare in his locker. Really? So where was it? Hadn't he brought it home to be washed? All the signs were there. She just hadn't been looking for them, or perhaps, on some subliminal level, she'd been ignoring them. And what a time to get dumped. Now she'd have to go to Christmas parties on her own, no romantic Christmas Eve meal out, no lovely Christmas presents on Christmas morning curled up in bed, pulling the duvet off each other and refusing to get up. Instead she'd have to go to her parents' in Oxfordshire. Why had they moved? Now she'd have a seven-hour train journey, if the trains were running. You could never tell in this country. If it snowed, chaos reigned; everybody forgot how to drive. Already two leaves on the track meant a cancelled train, so snowfall could mean having to stay home for days. She could imagine herself stuck on a railway siding near Preston as the passengers in the carriage sang Slade's 'Merry Christmas Everybody', and girls wore sexy Santa dresses and tinsel-covered deely boppers, whilst she sat po-faced, like Ebenezer Scrooge. Wonderful.

Wiping the tears from her face, Rebecca drew a pen and pad towards her and tried to work out if she would be able to keep her lovely flat.

Chapter Seven

3 December

The next day at nine o'clock sharp Natalie opened up the bakery. The aroma of the delicacies she had baked wafted through the shop and out into the street. The morning was bright again, but crisp and cool. Natalie didn't feel the cold at all, as she had been baking in the kitchen since six thirty and the ovens emitted plenty of heat.

At five past nine, the doorbell chimed. Jacob.

'Hi there, sorry if I'm a bit keen, but I just wondered if you'd heard anything yet.'

Natalie relayed to him the conversation with Mrs Williams and Jacob promised to get references to her within the hour. He had written references at home.

'Good,' said Natalie, 'And when you bring them, can you come in ready to work, too?'

'Absolutely,' he said, with a huge grin on his face.

Over the next hour Natalie got to meet a few more of Sugar and Spice's regulars and she chatted with the customers, making them want to stay and natter, so they ended up ordering another cup of tea, or having a cake when they hadn't intended to have one. By the time Jacob returned there was a queue almost out the door, and all the tables were filled.

'Just take the customers' orders for now and we'll grab a few minutes to go through the formalities when it's less busy,' Natalie advised, as she handed him a uniform to put on. 'For now, all you need to know is *wash your hands*.'

Jacob nodded, washed his hands in the sink behind the counter and immediately began serving customers, asking them to help him out when he didn't know the names of the cakes, managing not to infuriate them with his inexperience, by his lovely manner. Old ladies left the bakery full of praise for the young man who had been flung in at the deep end, and alongside a temporary new manager, too. The regulars were quietly happy.

When the rush was over, Natalie turned to Jacob and said, 'Thanks for that. Right, let's have a look at those references, shall we?' and, business-like, she put on her glasses and took from Jacob the envelopes he had retrieved from his jacket pocket.

'Well, that all seems in order,' Natalie said, after a few minutes of perusing the pages of A4 she had withdrawn from the envelopes. 'So, let me fill you in on what we do and what I need help with. It'll be a work in progress, as I'm still learning. This is only my second day.'

Jacob awaited further instructions.

'OK, can you bake?'

'No,' Jacob said flatly.

'Right, let's leave the baking to me, then. We can start with you serving customers and clearing tables. I'll show you how to use the coffee machine, for latte, mocha, espresso and the like. That'll be a big help, as making coffee can be quite time-consuming. I'd also like you to tell me when we're running low on any particular cakes, so I can try and make more, depending on what time of day it is. Make sense?'

'Yep, sounds good.'

'You can count, can't you? Without a calculator, I mean,' Natalie clarified.

'Yes, no problem.'

'Good. Well, I would suggest familiarising yourself with the price list. I'll talk you through the cakes we have here, as I gathered earlier you don't know the names of all of them.'

'About half,' Jacob admitted.

'No problem. By the end of the day, you'll know your way around a piece of pecan pie,' Natalie assured him.

As she ran through the cakes from left to right: angel cake, banana cake, bran muffins, banoffee pie, Battenberg cake, she realised Mrs Williams had alphabetised her layout. Natalie had no idea if it was intentional or not, but it made her giggle. Jacob looked at her oddly and she said, 'It's nothing,' then told him, since it would be easier for him to remember the names if he knew they were in alphabetical order. Plus, if he was to display the cakes in the glass cabinets, it would assist him in remembering what went where.

Just then another customer arrived, so their training session was cut short. Jacob chatted with the elderly gent, who was in for some Battenberg cake. After he left, Jacob laughed and said, 'Thank God he didn't ask for *zabaglione*!'

'Yes, we've got quite a bit of this alphabet to get through yet, and just so you know, we don't have any *zabaglione*.'

'Well, that's easy enough to remember. So where were we?'

'C. Carrot cake, chocolate cake,' she said, indicating each with a wave of her hand. 'D – date and walnut loaf and Dundee cake. E – Eccles cake. F – fondant fancy and fruit cake.' Natalie drew breath and stopped to ask Jacob which one was Eccles cake. He got it right. She continued, 'Genoa cake, gingerbread. No H, I, J or K and we go straight to L for lemon cake.'

'Straight to hell, did you say?' Jacob made an effort at humour.

'I hope your jokes improve,' Natalie said bluntly, but with a smile in her voice.

They got through discussing the rest of the cakes without mishap, stopping twice to serve customers. By the time the lunchtime rush arrived, Jacob was able to distinguish his Madeira cake from his upside-down cake.

He was a hit with the elderly ladies, charming them with his cornflower blue eyes and dirty blond hair, even if it was a little long for their tastes, so they confided to Natalie. Some of the regulars kept him busy asking for more tea, and he cleared tables whilst Natalie prepared new batches of the cakes that they were running low on. Mrs Gardiner, an elderly lady who they later discovered had never married, came in to meet Mrs Seymour once a week, to share a piece of cake, a pot of tea and a chinwag. Mrs Gardiner's guide dog, Sam, a seven-year-old golden Labrador with a gentle personality, lay at his owner's feet but remained always on the alert and pre-empted his owner's every move.

Natalie stood back for a moment and admired how the bakery café was filling up. Jacob was chatting with the latest customer, a young mum with a baby in a sling. She guessed the baby to be around four months old. The baby girl was trying to grab Jacob's finger, although her attention appeared to be temporarily distracted by the pink iced cakes he was packing into a bag for her mum.

The bakery's five tables were occupied. At table one were Mrs Gardiner and Mrs Seymour, table two had been nabbed by the young mum who had just come in; a changing bag sat atop it, a muslin cloth draped carelessly over the chair. At table three were three teenagers – Natalie welcomed teenagers, as long as they bought something and didn't cause any disruption. These kids were genuine, each scoffing a different type of muffin whilst simultaneously texting on their phones. Every so often they would giggle at something and hold their phones up to each other, laugh some more and then resume texting. Natalie had always thought she was pretty open-minded. She had seen a lot in her time, but this variant on conversation went against everything she had ever learned. But progress was progress, for good or for bad. Two young women, presumably in their late twenties, sat at table four. They were deep in conversation and only picked at their slices of carrot cake and sponge cake occasionally. At the final table sat a man with his laptop. He had been polite enough to ask if Natalie minded if he charged his laptop on the bakery's socket. 'As long as you're a paying customer, you can hoover up the electricity,' she'd said.

The man's relief was apparent and thanking Natalie, he said, 'I left my charger at home and I need to send my boss this report as soon as I finish it. It was due this morning. I've been typing faster, trying to finish it before my battery dies on me.'

'No problem. Now, what can I get you?' Natalie had said, waving her hand towards the bakery's offerings.

Everything was going OK so far, both the bakery and her project in general. Natalie had made contact with two of the four and had already been instrumental in Jacob getting a job, so things were heading in the right direction. He seemed a nice boy, too. She had chosen well. He was already proving to be a hard worker and a definite asset to the bakery. He'd upsold several customers who had only come in for a cup of tea, to tea and cake, commenting on the great opportunity to sit and enjoy the view from the bakery café.

The door opened again and a harried-looking girl rushed in, talking quickly into her mobile phone. 'Yes, Meredith, I've got it. I know what the order is. It's always the same. I'm not likely to forget.' Self-consciously, the girl brought her hand to her mouth, her eyes going wide. Recovering quickly, she said, 'Sorry, the line's breaking up. I'll see you when I get back,' and hung up. 'Phew!' she said, almost to herself, but Jacob heard her.

'Tough day?' he asked.

'Tough boss.'

'Oh dear. I know what you mean.' He winked at Natalie.

'Really?' she asked, 'I've always found Mrs Williams really nice.'

'Oh, not Mrs Williams, this one here. Battleaxe,' he confided in her.

Natalie turned away and stifled a laugh.

The girl studied Natalie, then said, 'Appearances can be deceiving. She seems...normal. My boss acts the part of superbitch. She makes Cruella De Vil look like Bambi's mother.'

Jacob burst out laughing. 'You're painting a great picture of her. Does she ever come in here, then, so I can make sure I go into hiding or take the day off?'

'No, she's "too busy" to do menial stuff like fetch her own cakes. That's why she sends me, her gopher.'

'Well, I'm glad she did send you. Sounds like I've had a right lucky escape. She might have skinned me and made me into a coat!'

The girl laughed. 'I'm Sophie. Can I have a slice of

carrot cake and a chocolate éclair, please?'

'Let me guess, the carrot cake is for your boss?'

'Yep. How did you guess?'

'Well, anyone who's that much of a bitch hasn't eaten our chocolate éclairs before. Carrot cake is much more boring, don't you think?' Jacob sounded convincing, even though he hadn't sampled any of the cakes himself yet – a real charmer.

Sophie put her head on one side, pondered this for a second and then said, 'You know what? You're so right. I can't believe I just spoke to Cruella like that. She'll probably shoot me on sight when I get back.'

'What did you say to her exactly?' asked Jacob, pretending he hadn't overheard her conversation.

'I was sarcastic to her, as she was her usual patronising self. I don't know what it is. She brings out the worst in me. I'm going to end up turning into her, I spend so much time with her.'

'God, I hope not.' Jacob said, clutching his heart in mock horror. 'She sounds dreadful. Buy an extra chocolate éclair and bribe her with that, if things get nasty,' he advised.

'You're joking, aren't you? Cruella, or rather, Meredith, thinks cream is the devil, although she actually believes carrot cake is *healthy*.'

'I don't think she's alone in that. Well, have a good day and I hope Cruella isn't too vicious to you. Oh, and I'm Jacob,' he added, as if realising somewhat belatedly that she had given him her name earlier but he hadn't reciprocated.

'Yes, you too. See you again,' said Sophie, giving him a little wave as she held open the door, allowing a lady in a wheelchair through.

Natalie spent the rest of the day weighing and measuring

ingredients and watching customers' ordering habits, to see how many of each cake she would need for the next day. Of course, it was only an indication, as every day would see different customers. She'd seen the glint in the eyes of not only the old ladies who she'd overheard thought Jacob a sweet boy, but also several schoolgirls, who had just about swooned when they saw him. Jacob had no idea he was such a hit, which was truly endearing.

The bakery closed at five thirty, having sold out of pretty much everything and having provided sanctuary for a pleasingly high number of customers in its café. Natalie had discussed takings and what the bakery usually achieved each day with Mrs Williams, and she was quietly confident that they were on target to match that. Not for the first time that day she wondered how poor Mrs Williams' operation had gone. It was never fun to be in hospital, but particularly not at that age. She supposed in a way, although she wasn't one of Natalie's chosen four, she was helping Mrs Williams by keeping her bakery open.

'Good first day?' Natalie asked Jacob, as he took off his uniform.

'Yes, I really enjoyed it. I loved talking to the customers and even though I haven't worked in a bakery before, I think I'm going to like it. I loved the buzz of all the people in the café, too.'

'Yes, that's something I've always really enjoyed; that and people watching,' Natalie agreed.

'I want to thank you for giving me a chance,' said Jacob. 'I don't mean to sound superior, but after studying for four years, I didn't expect to end up in a shop, but work is just so hard to find.'

'I know. I hear there are seventy applicants for every job and in this sector as many as two hundred.'

'It doesn't bear thinking about,' said Jacob, shaking his head. 'So, thanks again.'

'You're welcome. Now, you get off, have a nice evening and I'll see you tomorrow. Do you think you could come in at eight thirty, help me set up?'

'No problem. Have a good one.' Jacob took his jacket from the peg and left.

Natalie appraised the silent bakery, as she watched passers-by go about their business. It had been dark for over an hour now. Today had gone well. The pieces were starting to fall into place.

Chapter Eight

4 December

Jacob arrived at the bakery ahead of schedule next day. Natalie was juggling trays, so he bid her good morning and went to assist her. Taking Natalie's instructions on board from the day before, Jacob began to arrange the cakes and pastries on the platters in the glass cabinet. They smelled wonderful and his stomach rumbled. Natalie came up behind him just then to hand him another batch of cakes, and said, 'Haven't you had breakfast?'

'No, no time. I must have set my alarm wrong. It didn't go off.'

'Right, well, as soon as we're done with setting up, grab yourself a croissant or something and a cup of tea. I don't want you passing out mid-morning.'

'Thanks. I'll pay for it, of course.'

'No, you won't,' Natalie insisted. 'Right, I'm off to get the strawberry tarts.'

As he put them in the display case, Jacob marvelled at how many types of cakes there were and how Natalie managed to make them all herself without staying overnight in the bakery. *What time does she start in the morning?* Finished arranging the cakes, he unloaded the dishwasher and stacked the dishes on the shelves, then asked Natalie what needed to be done next. Natalie shouted through from the back, 'Nothing urgent. Just have some breakfast.'

So Jacob did as he was told, took a plate from the pile of dishes he had just unloaded, a *pain au chocolat* from the display case and made himself some coffee. He noticed the machine was already on. Natalie must have done it earlier; he knew industrial coffee machines could take a while to heat up. As he munched on his pastry and sipped his coffee, he thought about Natalie. She was a bit of an enigma. What must she be? Thirty-five, forty, but with the kindly way of a grandmother, or rather, what Jacob imagined a grandmother must be like. He had never known either of his, as they had both died before he was born.

Although Natalie had spent much of the previous day bustling back and forth between the kitchen and the front shop, Jacob had noticed her way with the customers. She always had a kindly word for them. She was interested. Chatting with the blind lady, she had told her that her dog had the most beautiful coat and asked her and her companion how long they had been coming here. She'd given the mum who had brought in the baby girl in the front-facing carrier, some recipes for when she got older – swore by them. The woman had been ever so grateful and promised to try them out and seemed pleased at having been given such attention. Jacob realised he had no idea if Natalie had children of her own, but he didn't want to pry. Women could be complex creatures, although he wasn't speaking from his own recent experience, he thought woefully. The chance of him getting a date was thin, even now that he had a job. Despite the pay Natalie had discussed with Mrs Williams being at the high end for a bakery assistant, it still really only covered essentials. He could maybe afford to take someone for a coffee, but that would be about it; the grand sum of his wooing efforts.

Natalie and he muddled along quite well as the bakery became busier. People were already starting to do their Christmas shopping, and the radio churned out the same songs as it did every year. Unsurprisingly Natalie, a jolly sort, Jacob thought, had the radio tuned constantly to stations playing Christmas songs. She was clearly a festive sort of person. Jacob had never enjoyed Christmas much. Christmas was for families and a time for them to spend it together. Well, that was the general idea, but that concept appeared to have passed his family by.

For a Wednesday, when many shops in the town closed for a half day, the bakery café was hearteningly full. The cold snap helped, as those who had braved the shops instead of ordering everything online entered the shop frozen stiff. Jacob had heard varying reports on the weather.

'A hard frost this morning, wasn't it?' 'I had to scrape my car windscreen today for the first time this year.' 'I'll need to dig out my gloves.' 'Must buy a new winter coat.' 'The sunshine's deceptive, isn't it?' 'Weather forecast said it might be below zero overnight.' 'Think I'll be wearing my thermals tonight.'

The bakery fortunately was a haven for those seeking refuge from the cold, with its ovens constantly emitting heat, as well as the café section being centrally heated.

At twelve thirty, the door tinkled once more and a familiar face appeared. Sophie.

Jacob grinned and said, 'Ah, so she didn't eat you alive then?'

Returning his smile, Sophie moved her windswept hair back from her face and said, 'Nope, I got away with it. I think she was distracted with too many other things. I did, however, display the spare chocolate éclair on my desk to wind her up, and she was practically salivating and giving me evils every time she walked past.'

'Sounds like you've got the measure of her.' Jacob laughed, his face lighting up.

Natalie looked on, the corners of her mouth twitching. Jacob had told her when they were closing up yesterday about Sophie's evil boss.

'So what can I get you today?' asked Jacob.

'I'm going to have some of that Rocky Road and the usual carrot cake for the Ice Queen.'

'Does she think she'll be able to see in the dark if she consumes it in vast quantities?' said Jacob, as he used tongs to lift out a slice of Rocky Road.

'I don't know about seeing in the dark, but she definitely seems to have eyes in the back of her head,' was Sophie's witty comeback. 'See you're busy again. Enjoying it?'

'Yes,' Jacob said, 'we've had a right good mix of people in and today everyone's trying to get out of the cold.'

'No wonder. It's brass monkeys out there.' Sophie shivered. 'Tell you what, stuff Meredith. It's *my* lunch hour. Can I have a latte, please? I'm going to grab a table and read my book for half an hour. You don't mind, do you, if I eat my sandwich here? I know I didn't buy it here…'

Jacob, unsure, cast a glance at Natalie, who nodded that it was fine. They didn't sell sandwiches anyway and Sophie was still a paying customer.

'Sure, grab a seat. I'll bring your coffee and cake over,' Jacob replied, as he placed the carrot cake in a bag and handed it to her.

'Thanks a lot.' Sophie ensconced herself in the corner table near the window, which an elderly couple had just vacated. She took out her e-reader and powered it up.

A few minutes later, Jacob brought her order and would

have stopped to chat, but a queue was forming again.

What a nice girl.

Jacob had served at least a dozen customers one after the other. He stopped to draw breath and wiped sweat from his brow with a handkerchief. Working in a bakery, he was discovering, was hard work and it was hot, even on the coldest day of the year so far. The ovens weren't so far away and the proximity to the coffee machines meant he was constantly boiling. He happened to glance up just as a girl came in, taking off her plum-coloured floppy velvet hat as she did so.

Jacob was struck dumb. She had a perfect rosebud mouth, heart-shaped face and porcelain skin, truly peaches and cream. Her hair cascaded down her back over her plum trench coat and he stood transfixed as she pulled off her gloves. The girl gazed around as if she had never been there before. Perhaps she hadn't, thought Jacob, who clearly wasn't in much of a position to know. Noticing him smiling at her, she made her way towards the counter.

'Hi. Can I have a pot of tea, please, Earl Grey, if you have it, and–' she cast her eye across the selection of cakes and pastries and came up with '–a slice of that chocolate fudge cake. Does it come with cream?'

'I can put some cream on it,' Jacob said.

'That would be great, thanks.'

Jacob signalled that he would bring it over and the girl went to grab a seat.

As Rebecca sat down, she spied a woman sitting at the table next to her, wearing a fabulous pair of black patent riding boots.

I must get a new pair, she thought. *I'll need to save up. No-one to buy me them as a Christmas present now;*

certainly not Ethan. She removed a newspaper from her bag, flipped to the Lettings page and began to read.

'Loch Rd. Modern luxury 2 bedroom unfurnished flat in the popular Winstanton area. Station ten minutes' walk away. £500 pcm.'

'Grange Avenue. Set in a lovely, quiet, residential and family area of Winstanton, this 2 bedroom unfurnished cottage apartment offers fantastic living accommodation. Unfurnished. Available now. £500 pcm.'

'Knap Lane. Spacious first-floor apartment, available unfurnished and comprising of spacious and bright lounge with balcony, newly fitted kitchen, 3 double bedrooms…' Rebecca stopped reading that one. She didn't need three bedrooms, there would only be her. Possibly there would always only be her. Sighing, she picked up a pen and tapped it against her lips as she read on,

'Barn Crescent. Offered to the market in good internal condition, this particularly spacious two bedroom ex-local-authority flat located in the Winstanton area…' Rebecca peered at the photo – ugh! She couldn't bring herself to live there. And why was everything at the top end of her budget? Five hundred pounds a month. She flicked through a few pages, glancing solely at prices before finally noticing a couple which were a little cheaper.

'Unfurnished, modern second-floor flat in popular residential area, close to local amenities and transport routes. Internally this property is in walk-in condition throughout and comprises lounge with dining area, modern kitchen, 2 double bedrooms and bathroom with shower. Further benefits include electric storage heating, double glazing, secure door entry system and parking. £395 pcm. Viewing is recommended.'

Now that sounds more like it, Rebecca thought, although

she pulled a face at the prospect of storage heaters. She and Ethan had replaced the storage heaters in their flat with gas ones and a new boiler, at considerable expense, as the storage heaters practically ate money. At least the double glazing would help keep the heating bills down. With energy costs constantly on the increase, it was important to make savings where possible. Listen to her, she sounded as if she was about eighty. That's what this split with Ethan had reduced her to; someone who talked, or thought, about the price of gas and electricity. £395. *What's wrong with the flat? Ah, no shower.* It hadn't even occurred to her that in the twenty-first century a rented flat could come without a shower; it didn't bear thinking about. She liked a bath as much as the next person, for a good long soak, in a cloud of foamy bubbles, but not for the ten minutes she had in her rush to get out the door every morning.

The secure door entry system was a big plus, as Rebecca was terrified of being burgled; it had happened to her years ago when she had lived in a ground-floor flat and an intruder had broken in during the night. She had disturbed him by getting up to go to the toilet. Fortunately, they hadn't come face to face, and the next morning it had become clear that he had escaped through the living room window. When Ethan and she had been together, she had felt so much safer in the knowledge he would be there every night, and gradually the fear had left her, but now it had returned. She had still insisted on installing an alarm when she moved in with him. Rental properties, at least flats, were unlikely to have burglar alarms.

Unbeknownst to Rebecca, as she perused the newspaper, Jacob whilst bustling around preparing her latte and cake, couldn't take his eyes off her. He knew he had a queue of customers to deal with, but somehow he needed to find out if this girl came in regularly, or if this was his one chance. Did he look presentable? Would it be bad business practice for him to ask for her number? All this ran through his head as he added the swirl to her latte and the cream to her cake.

'Be with you in just a second,' he said to the next person in line.

'I'll get it,' Natalie said, materialising behind him.

Phew, thought Jacob. That would give him some breathing space. He weaved his way around the tables, smiled at Sophie, who happened to glance up from her book just then, and set Rebecca's order in front of her.

'There you go. Can I get you anything else? Sugar, perhaps?'

'No, I'm fine, thanks.'

She's sweet enough, thought Jacob, catching himself just in time from voicing that.

Going for the brave approach, he dived in. 'I haven't seen you in here before.'

Clearly thinking he would have already been halfway back to the counter, Rebecca looked up from the property ads, frowned slightly and said, 'That's because today's my first visit.'

'Ah...' Jacob was stuck for what to say next, but managed to stammer out, 'Well, don't make it your last,' and gave her what he hoped was his least scary, non-stalkerish smile.

'I won't.' She smiled at him, then returned her attention to her newspaper.

What a beautiful girl, well spoken, too, but such sad eyes. Jacob wondered what was going on in her life that was making her so sad.

When he looked up, Sophie, at the next table, was

watching him, and for some reason he felt awkward.

Ten minutes later, Sophie said, 'Bye, Jacob. See you tomorrow.'

'Bye, Sophie, say hi to Cruella for me.'

They both laughed and the door chimed as Sophie left.

Once the lunchtime rush had died down, Jacob cleared tables and stacked the dishwasher. The girl was still there. As he cleared away Sophie's things, he lingered more than was necessary near the back of the girl's chair. She was reading the property section of the newspaper; *probably checking for houses to buy with her boyfriend*, he thought despondently.

Natalie, looking on, saw the change of expression on Jacob's face and allowed herself a slight smile. All was progressing nicely.

Rebecca had soon figured out, once she had started totting up the outgoings on her and Ethan's flat: mortgage, house insurance, council tax, utilities, as well as food and travel, that there was no way she could afford it on her own. Even if she lived the life of a nun and became teetotal, she would never manage it. And that wasn't including things like holidays or buying people presents, parking, haircuts, and all the other things that made up her budget. Ethan, having a more highly paid job than her, she knew, would buy her out, and although she wasn't best pleased with him at the moment – the understatement of the century – she knew he'd give her a fair deal. But she couldn't stay in the flat indefinitely, although he hadn't pressed her yet.

She didn't know where he was staying, as their rare communication was either by text or e-mail. At some point they would have to sit down and talk to each other about the flat. She was dreading dividing up the items they had bought together. She remembered that, unfairly, Ethan had made her sell some of her furniture when they had moved in together as he preferred his: his fridge freezer, his sofa, his king-size bed. Now she would have the added cost of having to replace those items. The sums she had received for her stuff had been paltry compared with what she had paid for them and what they would cost to buy again. At least renting she wouldn't have that outlay for a while. If things weren't so bad at work, she would have brazened it out and asked for a raise. It's not as if she wasn't due one; she hadn't had a raise in three years. Cuts. Yes, always cuts.

She'd been Art Assistant to the Art Director at Feathers Gallery in Aberfoyle for three years now; her first job after university. The pay was poor, although she enjoyed the work, most of the time. She loved the exhibitions and took great pride in her part in arranging them, creating the buzz for them, even down to writing the invitations. She knew her boss felt she was indispensable, but he wasn't in a position to offer her any more money, as times were tough in the industry right now. Henry, her boss, was a dear, sweet man, who many often mistook for being gay, due to the timbre of his voice and his eclectic wardrobe, but the truth was, he was on his third marriage and had six children. So she quite understood that when pickings were meagre, the purse strings had to be tightened. She did wonder sometimes how he afforded an assistant at all. She knew she did much more than a normal assistant did; she was Henry's right-hand woman and he told her often enough, but it didn't put any extra pennies in her pay packet, which didn't help her current financial situation one bit.

Rebecca took out her phone and texted her best friend, Hannah. *'Hi. How u? Up for a bit of flat-hunting with me at the weekend?'*

Deciding that she'd had enough of perusing information on flats, Rebecca embarked upon another task which couldn't be put off. Usually she loved making a list of the Christmas presents she needed to buy, but this year she took no delight in it. At least she would have one less person to buy for, she thought with a pang.

She'd have to cut back on presents, too. Hopefully, her family and friends would understand. Hannah, thankfully, was already taken care of. She'd bought her tickets to see Rainy Parade, back in August, when they'd first gone on sale. *Phew!* They'd set her back sixty quid, so she breathed a sigh of relief she wasn't having to pay for them now. Carefully, she wrote her list in the little notebook she carried everywhere with her. She liked to sketch ideas or jot down notes for exhibitions, so always having a notebook to hand was a prerequisite for her.

Mum – pyjamas; her mum was easy to buy for as she liked to have new Christmas PJs.

Dad – 3-month streaming subscription. Her parents didn't have satellite TV, nor did they go to the cinema, so this was a good bet. Her dad loved action and disaster films. He was never happier than when watching a good film featuring an earthquake or an avalanche.

Grampa – jumper - preferably from The Woollen Mill. He loved those.

As Rebecca wrote her list, she found herself feeling lighter; even though it would affect her bank balance and not improve her finances, she allowed herself to revel a little in the season of the year.

By the time she left the café an hour later, she felt

happier. When the guy who had served her earlier said, 'Hope to see you again soon,' she'd smiled at him and said without hesitation, 'You will.'

Chapter Nine

5 December

'Oh for God's sake, I feel like crap, too, and I'm here!'
Meredith coughed into her mobile phone.

'I'm sorry, Meredith, but I can't stop throwing up and...'

'I don't want to hear the details. Just make sure you're
in here tomorrow. We have the Xanders presentation in the
afternoon and I have a huge list of things I need you to do.
Make sure you're on e-mail later.' And with that Meredith
hung up.

Sophie pulled the bucket closer to her bed, grabbed
some tissues from a box on her bedside table and wiped
her brow, which was soaked in sweat. She had a fever, she
was sure of it. She'd check her temperature shortly, but
right now, she needed to rest. Within two minutes, she was
fast asleep again.

Today of all days. Meredith's talons flew across her
keyboard, bringing up her schedule. Something would
need to be cancelled. She couldn't do everything planned
for today without Sophie here to do the donkey work.
Meredith would never admit it to Sophie, but she depended
on her – a lot. There, Pritchards, a small engineering
company in Glasgow. They would do – repeat business.

She would sweet-talk them and rearrange for next week. She sifted through the rest of her diary and accessed Sophie's computer for files she knew she would need for the day's meetings. Glancing at her watch, she saw she had only ten minutes before her first video conference call with the US. *Bloody girl!*

At Sugar and Spice Natalie was baking Christmas cakes. She thought she'd introduce Christmas gradually. Some people didn't like Christmas shoved in their face until the traditional twelve days before, but others, like herself, would happily have Christmas music playing and Christmas decorations up all over the place from the beginning of the month. In the past Natalie had done just that in her own home. Today she'd chosen a chocolate and cinnamon Bundt cake and sliced it up into generous but not off-putting slices. Already she had formulated a list in her head of how her Christmas cakes would roll out right up until Christmas Eve. She hoped they would be a hit with the bakery's clientele and was sure Mrs Williams wouldn't mind, as long as the bakery was making money. Natalie had also brought a holly wreath with her for the shop. As she'd passed the garden centre on the way home the night before, she'd seen a sign saying *'Holly wreaths £10'*, so she had decided that would be Sugar and Spice's first Christmas decoration.

The doorbell chimed and a woman came in, shaking snow off her boots. There had been a light dusting overnight which had turned heavier that morning. As a result, fewer customers had ventured in, although it was still early. Natalie vowed if it continued like this, her Bundt cake wouldn't go to waste. She would give it to the homeless, or those selling that magazine, *The Big Issue*.

'Morning,' the woman greeted Natalie. She seemed the hearty type, and the fact she had braved the weather conditions when most wouldn't, bore testimony to that.

'Good morning. What can I get you?' Natalie asked. Jacob was out of the bakery for a few minutes, as Natalie had asked him to go and buy some newspapers since their delivery hadn't arrived. Mrs Williams always displayed the newspapers on a rack so that patrons could pass the time reading whilst they ate and drank their purchases.

'I was wondering if I might ask a favour. We're selling raffle tickets for the old folks' home and pensioners' club. Would you be interested in buying some?'

'Sure,' said Natalie. 'How much are they?'

'A pound each for a book of five.'

Natalie took three pound coins from her purse and gave them to the woman, a well-meaning sort.

'Thanks ever so much. Could I impose a little more and ask if you'd mind trying to sell them in the bakery? It would mean ever so much to the old folks if they could have a Christmas party. There was no money in the budget this year, hence the fundraiser.'

'How many do you have? I can take fifty books of five to start. Do you have a contact number and I'll let you know if I need more?' Natalie asked.

The woman, who then introduced herself as Cathy, was delighted and readily handed over the requested number of raffle tickets. 'That really is marvellous. You've been such a help. Here's my number.'

Natalie took the piece of paper offered her and then said, 'Just out of interest, what do they do at the pensioners' club?'

'Well,' said Cathy, 'they play dominoes, cards and bingo, they read and do the crossword, and they have lunch there, as well as being read to from that day's newspaper and using the headlines as talking points.'

'Hmm,' Natalie said. 'Do you have any leaflets about it?'

'Yes, I do, somewhere.' Cathy rooted around inside the voluminous pockets of her Barbour jacket and brought out a small sheaf of pale green flyers. She passed one to Natalie, who quickly read it. It reiterated everything Cathy had just said.

'Perhaps your raffle will do better if I put a leaflet up inside the café, too. The club sounds very good. We get quite a few elderly people in here. It could be right up their street.'

'Let's hope so. I'm terribly sorry–' Cathy glanced at her watch '–but I'm late for picking up my granddaughter. It's been nice talking to you, and good luck with the tickets.'

'Thanks and I think we'll manage to sell all the tickets,' Natalie confided to her.

'Good, good, well, must crack on. Bye.'

Jacob returned just then with a selection of newspapers. He asked Natalie if she wanted to read one whilst it was quiet, but she said no, she was off to work on another idea for a Christmas cake. Jacob shook his head. He couldn't work out what all the fuss was over Christmas.

'Nice holly wreath, by the way,' he noted.

'Oh, I saw them for sale near my cottage last night, so thought it might help spur us on with the start of the season.'

'Hmm,' Jacob replied, unconvinced. 'What are you doing?'

'Putting up a leaflet about the pensioners' club and old folks' home. We're going to be selling raffle tickets for them.'

'Well, I'll have a book of five,' Jacob said, when Natalie had finished explaining to him how it worked. 'I'm a bit low on cash right now to buy any more, but I'll do my best to shift the others.'

'That's the spirit. Right, what do you think?' Natalie asked, as she stood back to admire the green leaflet she'd put up.

'Prominent, no-one will miss it there.'

'Good, that was the plan. Oh, here's another customer.'

Interestingly, it was Stanley.

'Good morning, Stanley, come in and sit yourself down. You must be frozen.'

Jacob observed the old man; he did look very stiff, and moved with some difficulty.

'I needed some essentials: bread, milk, that kind of thing. I'd completely run out.'

Natalie helped him off with his coat, which she hung up for him.

'Here, sit at this table, next to the radiator,' she suggested.

Slowly, Stanley lowered himself into the chair.

'Now, what can we get you?'

'I'd love some tea, please, and what cakes have you today? You had so many different ones the other day when I was in.'

'Jacob, could you make Mr Winters some tea, please?'

'Coming right up.' Jacob hopped to it. *Poor old man.* Jacob dreaded the thought of getting old. Mr Winters looked as if everything was a real effort.

Natalie never forgot a name. Jacob didn't know how she did it, but he found it quite charming, caring, and he envied her a little. He tried his best to remember everyone's name, but without meaning to be rude, many of the elderly people looked the same to him. They all tended to wear the same type of clothes and the women often had similar haircuts and even colours.

Replying to Stanley's question about the cakes, Natalie beamed at him and said, 'I've just made a cinnamon and chocolate Bundt cake. Would you like to try it? It's the first of my Christmas-themed cakes.'

'Well, yes, that sounds very nice, thank you.'

'Would you like a newspaper over?' Natalie asked.

'Yes, thanks. Which ones do you have?'

Natalie explained the choices and Stanley chose a well-known broadsheet which covered most of the table.

Happy that he appeared warm enough and content, Natalie returned to behind the counter to prepare his cake. She passed Jacob, who was bringing out his tea on a tray.

'There you go, Mr Winters.' Jacob set the tea in front of him, complete with silver sugar bowl and a ceramic milk jug.

'Thanks, son. So, are you enjoying your job, then?'

'I am, thanks. Everyone's been really nice and Natalie—' he winked at him '—is a sweetheart.'

'Yes, she has a lovely way about her.'

'She does, doesn't she? Well, I'll leave you to your paper. Oh, would you like to buy a raffle ticket for the pensioners' club?'

'What's that, son?'

Jacob pointed to the leaflet behind Stanley's head.

Stanley turned. 'Oh, I don't have my reading glasses on. What does it say?'

So Jacob read it out to him and noticed the expression change on Stanley's face.

'I didn't know we had such a thing in Winstanton,' Stanley said. 'It sounds very good, and what a pity they aren't going to have a Christmas party. Of course I'll buy a raffle ticket.'

'So you don't go to the club, Mr Winters,' Jacob said.

'No.'

'It sounds quite good, though, good place to meet people and they have lots of activities by the sounds of it,' said Jacob, taking an interest in the old man. *He's lonely,* Jacob thought. He wondered, as he had begun to do about people since working at Sugar and Spice, what the old man's story was.

'Yes, it does. Does it say which days they meet?'

'Erm, let me see. Yes, every day, by the looks of it.'

'What about how much it costs?' Stanley asked next.

'Doesn't say,' Jacob confirmed after scanning the leaflet, then rereading it thoroughly. 'I'm sure we could find out for you though.'

'Oh, I wouldn't want to put you to any bother, son.'

'It's no problem. We're hardly rushed off our feet today, are we?'

Stanley glanced around the almost empty café; he was their only customer. 'Well, that's true. I suppose no-one wants to come out in this foul weather if they don't have to.'

'And who can blame them?' Jacob said, as he put away some cutlery. 'Let me just ask Natalie if she knows.'

He returned a few minutes later.

'Natalie says she doesn't know but she has the phone number of the lady who was fundraising for them. She's going to give her a call.'

'Oh, I'm being such a nuisance.'

'Not at all. How's your cake?'

'Delicious,' Stanley said after devouring another mouthful. 'I've never had this bun cake before.'

'Bundt cake,' Natalie corrected him gently as she came into the café. 'I've just spoken to the organiser and she says it's every day and it's free if you're over seventy-five.'

'I definitely qualify for that,' joked Stanley.

'It's next to the old folks' home. They have a separate wing which houses some rooms where the club is set up.'

'Well, that gives me something to look forward to, then,' Stanley said between mouthfuls of cake. 'This really is lovely, hen.'

'Thank you, I'm so glad you're enjoying it. It means I'm doing something right.' Natalie smiled at him.

Stanley drank his tea, deep in thought. Maybe he would try out the club. He wouldn't be using gas and electricity when he was out. His heating could be on low and save him some money. The fuel bills were becoming increasingly more difficult to manage and he'd begun wearing two jumpers on a day like this, over his thermals. Nothing to lose really.

And he could be doing with the company. He hadn't really had many friends of his own, by the time Edie died. Most of his friends had preceded Edie to the grave; it was terrible to be one of only a few left. Maybe he would have something in common with the people there. Edie would have urged him to go, if she was still here.

By the time Stanley was leaving, the bakery had only had a sprinkling of customers. He asked for his bill and then called Jacob back, as he said it was incorrect.

'Oh, I'm sorry, let me check with Natalie.'

'No, son, I mean you've charged me too little. You haven't charged me for the cake.'

'Oh right, give me a minute.'

Jacob came back and said, 'Natalie says you're the first to taste her Bundt cake and guinea pigs get it free, so it's just the tea you're paying for today.'

'Oh, that's very kind.' His face lit up. Sometimes people's kindness made him a little emotional.

Stanley left the bakery feeling so much brighter, stronger and full of purpose than when he had woken up that morning. He'd never liked winter much anyway, despite his surname, but as he aged he liked it even less, and now with his Edie gone, he downright loathed the season. He didn't even have her little warm body to cuddle into at night.

He made up his mind to check out the club the next day, unless he was snowed in. Edie would be proud of him.

There was still the usual mad rush at lunchtime, as workers came in to get some cake and takeaway coffee, but Natalie saw a definite dropping off in the café clientele, presumably due to the weather. No matter, they'd recoup any downturn later, she knew. For now, she simply had to allow her plan to gain momentum.

At two fifteen, after the lunchtime rush had come and gone, the door chimed to reveal an immaculately dressed woman with knee-high black leather boots with what Natalie presumed to be a four-inch heel, and a sable-coloured coat, which if Natalie hadn't known better, she would have thought was the real thing. The woman, whose alabaster skin tone almost matched the snow outside, regarded the empty café with disdain and gave an audible sniff, as she pulled off her leather gloves.

'Can I help you?' Natalie asked, her usual broad smile on her face.

'Yes, a latte and a slice of carrot cake,' she barked, without so much as a please.

Taken aback by her tone, Jacob raised an eyebrow at

Natalie, out of the woman's line of sight.

Natalie smiled and said, 'To go or to sit in?'

The woman regarded Natalie as if she was a cretin and said with a hint of scorn, 'To go,' as if nothing could be further from her mind than having her coffee and cake on the premises.

Not to be beaten, Natalie persisted. 'I haven't seen you in here before.'

Rolling her eyes as if irritated by Natalie's small talk, she declared, 'That's because I've never been here before.'

'Oh right, and you chose today, in this terrible weather to give us your patronage for the first time. How nice of you.'

The woman narrowed her eyes at Natalie, then said, 'Not by choice, I assure you. My damned assistant called in sick with flu; useless girl. She usually fetches my order.'

'Ah, you mean Sophie,' said Natalie, 'Lovely girl, sorry to hear she's unwell. I hope she feels better soon.'

Cruella, or rather Meredith, stared at her. Natalie guessed Meredith was trying to calculate how well she knew Sophie and if that meant Sophie was spending longer than she should be in the café.

'Yes, well, she'll be back tomorrow.'

'Oh nothing serious, then. That's a relief.'

'I don't know what's wrong with her, but we have a big presentation tomorrow, so she'll be in if she wants to keep her job.' Meredith dropped the coins on the counter when Natalie mentioned how much it was and without waiting for her change, stalked off.

'I can't believe Cruella was here!' said Jacob, as they watched Meredith's figure retreat down the street. 'Charming, wasn't she? Sophie wasn't wrong there, then.'

'Ah, it's not always that simple,' Natalie said sagely. 'An angry and unhappy woman. Who would like to be her?'

'Not me, that's for sure,' said Jacob.

'So, are you going to help me eat this Bundt cake, then?' Natalie arched an eyebrow at Jacob, her cake slice at the ready.

'Why not? They're hardly beating a path to our door, and Mr Winters enjoyed it.'

'Ah, he was just being kind. Lovely old man. I think he's lonely. His wife died earlier this year. Christmas must be a hard time for him.'

'That's a shame, and yes, I imagine it won't be easy for him this year. Does he have any family?'

'I didn't get that far. One of the elderly ladies mentioned it in passing just after he left last time.'

They sat down to eat their cake and drink their tea.

'I hope he goes to the club,' said Jacob.

'Me too. I think he could do with the company.'

Meredith sat back down at her desk, fuming. *Bloody girl, and flavour of the month over at the bakery.* She barely tasted her carrot cake as she was so wound up. Afterwards, she remembered the array of delicious cakes in the bakery and resolved that occasionally she would go herself. It would give Sophie time to e-mail something or print off another report. She, Meredith, could get out of the office and stretch her legs, choose one of the other cakes. She scarcely had time to remember her own name most days, never mind spend ten minutes deliberating over which cake to choose. She could have, and perhaps should have, sent one of her other minions out to get her order, but the truth was, she hated delegating. She only trusted Sophie to do things right. Meredith continued to batter the keys on her laptop as if they were her mortal enemy until her receptionist announced her final meeting of the day.

Chapter Ten

6 December

Sophie felt terrible. Her whole body seemed to have gone into shutdown. She could barely move, yet that bitch Meredith had made it quite clear she had better be there for the presentation today. She was much worse than yesterday but she couldn't afford to lose her job, so she dragged herself out of bed, stood under a hot shower for a good twenty minutes and then applied enough make-up so that she couldn't be mistaken for someone in their death throes.

'I see you've graced us with your presence,' Meredith said sarcastically, turning on her heel, expecting Sophie to follow. Sophie shot Meredith a look which could have killed her if she'd turned around.

As Sophie took off her coat, Meredith barked instructions at her. Generally Sophie was like a sponge and could absorb multiple details with ease, but today she was fuzzy and her brain felt woolly. She had difficulty just functioning, yet Meredith was doing her usual, rat-a-tatting orders at her. She felt like telling her to f*** off, but stopped herself just in time, but oh, how satisfying it would be. If only she didn't need this job…

Stanley stood outside the old folks' home, unsure, now that he was here, that he would be brave enough to go in. He was a shy man really, and what if they were all nuts? What if it was full of people with mental illness and degenerative diseases? Naturally he felt for them, but he wasn't at that stage. He didn't want to go to use the toilet and find a woman sitting with the door open and her pants around her ankles.

His decision was soon made for him as Cathy, the fundraiser, arrived behind him and said, 'Here for the club, are we? Good stuff. In you go, you'll have a great time. Angus and George will be there already, if I'm not mistaken; always the early birds.'

Stanley stood, his mouth agape, then meekly preceded Cathy into the building. She ushered him down a corridor until they entered a large, airy room, with a vaulted ceiling. The building had originally been listed and had previously belonged to the church. True enough, two men sat playing cards: rummy.

'This is Angus,' Cathy said, indicating a portly gentleman of around seventy wearing a heavy cable-knit navy sweater and grey trousers.

'Hello.' Angus raised his hand in greeting, careful to shield his cards from them all.

'And this is George.' Cathy pointed out the other man, who wore an immaculate white shirt with a chocolate-coloured waistcoat, and trousers of a slightly lighter shade. The most notable feature about him was his enormous handlebar moustache, which gave him the air of a sergeant major.

'Nice to meet you.' George shook his hand; such a firm grip, Stanley noticed.

'I'm Stanley,' he almost whispered, then louder,

'Stanley Winters.'

'Winters, is it? That's a great name for now, with all this snow.' George let out a hearty laugh.

Stanley smiled, 'Aye, it is.'

'So, do you play rummy?' Angus asked him.

'It's been a while, but I did play, back in the day.'

'When was the day?' cackled George, easily amused.

'I often ask myself that, but I think I've decided now is the day.'

'Oh, this should be interesting. Were you any good?' asked Angus.

'I wasn't bad,' Stanley admitted. 'Above average.'

'Oh well, we like a bit of competition here, don't we, George?'

'Aye, we do that. Sorry, just a sec. Have to get important matters sorted first. Cathy?' George beckoned her over. 'What's for lunch today?'

'It's pea or lentil soup and then roast beef Stirlingshire with roast potatoes, parsnips and baby carrots, or gammon steak, pineapple and fried egg.'

'Ooh, I do like the roast beef.' Angus licked his lips.

'Yes, but they don't serve the food hot enough for my liking,' George grumbled.

'Well, at least they're heating the plates up now, as per your request,' Angus pointed out.

'Small mercies,' George conceded.

'The food's good,' Angus said, 'but I agree with George, I'd like it a bit warmer. We think someone sued them in the past for burning their tongue on their lunch.' Angus laughed at his own comment.

'Aye,' said George. 'It was probably on *Scotland Today – Pensioner burns tongue.*' The pair of them had a fit of the giggles, as Stanley looked on, bemused.

'So, Stanley, tell us a wee bit about yourself before the others arrive. We like to be in the know.'

Happy to have made two acquaintances already, Stanley settled back in his chair and shared a few snippets of his life with the two men.

Bustling around, trying to get everything ready for the club, Cathy came into the hall and saw that the three men were deep in conversation. As she'd been asked, Cathy dialled the number she'd been given, waited for the person on the other end to pick up, then introduced herself and said, 'Stanley's here and I think he's going to be just fine.'

Natalie thanked Cathy, replaced the receiver, and allowed herself a Cheshire Cat-like smile.

Fortunately the presentation went exceptionally well. Sophie somehow held her part together, even though she felt she might faint at any minute, and by the end of the meeting, contracts had been verbally agreed. For some in this business a handshake was enough; with others weeks passed waiting for approvals to go through. Sophie couldn't fault Meredith's presentation, just as Meredith couldn't fault Sophie's research. They would achieve so much more if Meredith wasn't such a control freak, an out-and-out bitch, and if she actually valued her. If she didn't thank her for today and for coming in when she clearly wasn't fit to work, Sophie would be job-hunting come the New Year.

She was happy to be sent out to the bakery today for two reasons. Firstly she wanted to get away from Meredith. As she walked the short distance from the office, Sophie thought with a smile of the other reason.

A woman with a buggy was struggling to open the door to Sugar and Spice when Sophie arrived.

'I'll get that for you,' she said, going ahead of the woman, opening the door and giving her baby boy a big smile and a 'Hello, handsome,' as they passed her.

It was such a relief to be out of the office and Sophie was glad the presentation was over. Everything for months had been building up to it and now they had won the contract. If Meredith were a normal boss, they'd be cracking open the champagne and celebrating. But all Meredith did was tell her to go to the bakery, although unusually she had asked for caramel shortcake – deviating from her habitual carrot cake.

Maybe she's lightening up – yeah, right.

Jacob smiled when he saw Sophie come in. He had been wondering if she was feeling better, as he enjoyed talking to her and was keen to let her know he'd met Cruella. When she turned to face the counter, he almost gasped. She looked terrible. Her eyes were sunken, had dark shadows under them and she was wheezing.

'I heard you were sick. You don't sound better to me,' Jacob said to Sophie, concern apparent in his voice.

'I'm not, I feel dreadful, but we had this really important presentation today and I wasn't able to get out of it.'

'Can I take it Cruella made you come in?'

'Yes, did you meet her? Lovely, isn't she?' Sophie coughed into a handkerchief. 'Sorry, I'll be out of here as quick as I can,' she said, seeing the worried glance from the mother with the baby.

'She was quite something,' Jacob agreed, 'charm personified. It was clear she missed you,' he said loyally.

'I'll bet. More like she missed her gopher.'

'That's probably true,' said Jacob. 'She really is a piece of work, a nasty woman altogether.'

'Anyway, what did you do to her? She's asked for caramel shortcake instead of her usual carrot cake.'

'Nothing. I didn't speak to her. It was Natalie who dealt with her.'

'Well, I don't know what she said or did to her, but the fact she's ordered something different is proof she can change. Where's Natalie? Can you ask her to talk to her again? Maybe Meredith will stop being a bitch!'

'I don't think her powers are that far-reaching.' Jacob laughed. 'But I'll let her know about the positive impact she's had on Meredith's ability to choose cakes.'

'Do, please. This is a real breakthrough,' Sophie said, as Jacob handed her the cakes and she took out her purse. 'OK, better get back to it. See you on Monday, unless Cruella has me in over the weekend. God, I hope not.'

'Get some rest, and hope you feel better,' Jacob called after her as Sophie left the bakery.

Thank God that's over, thought Meredith, breathing a sigh of relief. Sophie had come through for her, as she'd known she would. She knew the girl looked awful and she had told Sophie to touch up her make-up before the presentation started, to try to hide the dark circles around her eyes. She couldn't have her in the boardroom resembling someone from The Corpse Bride. And that terrible cough – well, she had an awful cough, too, but she managed to hide it, so she'd warned her to minimise the coughing.

The Xanders board had lapped up everything she told them, and she had known they would award her company the contract by the time she reached slide three. She really did leave nothing to chance. What she lacked in her personal life, she made up for in her professional one. She'd buy a more expensive bottle of wine tonight to celebrate. The adrenalin coursing through her veins made her feel temporarily better. Sophie wasn't the only one who was feeling unwell.

Meredith picked up her mobile and rang Amelia's number. She liked to keep her sister apprised of her success.

Chapter Eleven

7 December

'Are you sure this is the address?' Hannah asked Rebecca, eyeing the building uncertainly. Piles of rubbish lay outside; clearly the binmen hadn't been for a few weeks. An old car with stuffing coming out of its leather seats lay at one end of the front garden, and four cats, no five, swaggered around the outside of the building as if staking claim to it.

Rebecca was terrified of cats. 'I can't go in there. We'll have to phone and cancel.'

'Somehow I don't think it was going to be for you, anyway,' Hannah said.

They drove immediately round to the next viewing, which was an open house. A few other viewers milled around, murmuring to each other about what they liked and disliked. At least this one didn't look scary at first sight. Yes, it would need a little TLC, but for the most part it ticked all the boxes: it was under five hundred pounds a month, was furnished, and was relatively clean. The view out to the slagheap wasn't the most attractive, mind you.

The next property initially seemed OK, but then Rebecca noticed an odd smell. As she sat on the sofa, she noticed something flutter past her feet. A moth? She couldn't stand moths. Hannah lifted up one of the sofa cushions. It was riddled with dead moths. Rebecca ran out of the house. Hannah found her throwing up into a patch of snow.

'How can these properties be so misrepresented online? Not one of them is habitable.'

'Well, the one before the moth-infested one was OK.' Hannah tried to be fair.

'Don't. Don't mention this visit again, ever, or I might be sick again.'

The next property was in the centre of town, so Rebecca parked her Citroen Saxo, and she and Hannah climbed the stairs to the second-floor flat. It was a new build, higher in price than she had hoped to spend, but after this morning's nightmares, Rebecca was prepared to view anything, even stately homes and castles.

The rooms were small, but clean and brand new. Rebecca couldn't say she'd warmed to the place the way she had her own flat. It was neutral, so she'd be able to put her own stamp on it, although if she did go ahead with renting it, she'd have to ask in advance if she'd be allowed to modify anything. Most landlords, she understood, were happy to let you decorate or remodel as long as you put things back the way they were originally, before you moved out, or if you were improving the property.

Deciding she had had enough for one morning and since they were in the centre of town anyway, Rebecca suggested to Hannah that they nip into Sugar and Spice to try one of the cakes.

'Seriously, they're to die for, and there's a sweet guy there who's right up your street.'

'Sweet,' said the unattached Hannah. 'Does that mean he's as ugly as sin?'

'Not at all, the exact opposite, quite a hunk.'

'Lead the way.' Hannah pushed her friend forward, promise of a good-looking man apparently reason enough for her.

As they entered the bakery, Rebecca saw that it was much busier than during the week. The café was full, not a single free table. Just as she turned to head back out, wondering where else they could go that wasn't too far a walk, she heard a voice say, 'Table number five's free now,' and turning, she saw the boy from the other day smiling at her.

'Thanks.' She grinned at him. 'Hannah, over by the window. That couple's just leaving.'

Hannah nabbed the table, whilst Rebecca headed over to grab a menu, as she saw that the one on their table was missing.

'Do you have a menu?' she asked Jacob.

'Sure. So you live and work round here?' he asked.

'Yes, well, for now,' she said ruefully. Who knew what would happen once she had to sell her share of the flat to Ethan. He'd texted her the other night asking how the flat-hunting was going. *Giving me plenty of time to move, my arse.*

'Ah, it's just I've noticed the Saturday crowd is different to the people we see during the week.'

'Right,' said Rebecca, unsure where this was heading. 'We'll have a quick look at the menu and we'll be ready to order soon.'

'No problem. Take your time.'

The longer she stays in the café the better, thought Jacob. She looked different today, not dressed for work, but still very elegant in slim black trousers, a white fluffy jumper and black ankle boots. This trend of oversized boots costing hundreds of pounds, which had cropped up in the past few years, had never appealed to him, plus Jacob thought it made all the girls look the same. Rebecca's style was original and he liked it.

'Here's the menu. There are loads of cakes listed on it, but to be honest, you're better just to go up and see for yourself,' Rebecca told Hannah, as she swept her hair back from her face, where it had fallen over her eyes when she bent down to pick up her bag.

They chose their drinks and Rebecca told Hannah she wanted an Empire biscuit, 'Makes me feel like I'm back at school, but these Empire biscuits are nothing like the stodgy ones we had there.'

'You've no class,' her friend chided. 'I was going to have a *pain au raisin*, but I think I'll go for the Cake of the Day.'

'Ooh, what's that? I didn't see that,' Rebecca said, peering at the menu.

'No, I saw it up on the blackboard there, under Specials.'

'Oh right.' Rebecca squinted to read, as she wasn't wearing her contact lenses. She could drive fine without her contacts, but reading small print was a bit of a challenge.

'*Stollen*. Ah, German Christmas cake. Oh yeah, I'm definitely having that, then. I can have an Empire biscuit anytime.'

Rebecca went up to place their order and then sat down to analyse the morning's events.

'So, what are you going to do?' Hannah asked her.

'The only one that's even a possible is the new build, but it's the top end of, if not over, my budget, and tiny.'

'And how many more are on your list?'

'Two more this afternoon and that's about it unless I

want to change area. I don't.'

'And have you talked to Ethan?' Hannah asked, as she rotated a coaster between her middle finger and thumb.

'No, just by text. He's prepared to buy me out if I want him to, otherwise we put it on the market.'

'And what about all your stuff?'

'I'm putting off that conversation for as long as possible.' Rebecca was tearful; it wouldn't be a pleasant task.

Jacob brought over their order, set it down on the table, and said, 'Is there anything else I can get you, ladies?'

Ladies. What a charmer! But he's a nice guy. 'How about a decent flat in this area?' Rebecca asked.

Jacob's eyes went wide for a second, then he said, 'How many bedrooms?'

'One or two.'

'Any other requirements?' he mimicked estate-agent parlance.

'Parking, a shower and it's to rent, not buy.'

'Well, I don't know of any, but I'll keep my ear to the ground for you.'

'Thanks,' Rebecca said. *He's just being nice.*

Rebecca and Hannah discussed her separation from Ethan in hushed tones whilst they ate their *stollen* and drank their coffees.

Natalie watched the girls from a distance and thought happily to herself that all was on schedule.

The blare of a horn woke Meredith from a deep slumber next morning. She'd only fallen asleep properly around four. So much for celebrating. When she had arrived home the night before, after picking up a bottle of *Barbera d'Alba* reserve, she felt much worse than earlier. She was shivering and somehow she didn't think it was solely down to the sub-zero temperatures outside. Damn, she'd better not have flu; there was too much to do.

She had phoned out for a Chinese; she couldn't face making anything, no matter if it only required pinging in the microwave. Anyway, she needed comfort food and she was celebrating, so why not? To try to heat herself up, she took a shower, but although it helped at the time, within half an hour she was freezing again. She ate little of the Chinese and drank only half a glass of wine before calling it a night and going to bed, first throwing a second duvet on top.

About an hour after going to bed, the second duvet had been thrown off and Meredith had eventually thrown off the other duvet, leaving herself only partially covered by a thin sheet; her body was bathed in sweat. Dragging herself out of bed, she made a lemon drink with paracetamol before seeking refuge under the covers once more, where she tossed and turned for hours.

Meredith opened her eyes with difficulty; her eyelids seemed to be stuck together, her throat felt dry and her breathing was raspy. Gradually she pulled herself up to a sitting position. Christ, she felt awful. She'd never felt this bad before. Bloody flu. Just as well she had nothing urgent to do today, and it was Saturday. Thank God the presentation had been yesterday. Meredith managed to make it to the bathroom before a coughing fit overtook her. She must have what Sophie had. Bloody girl. A nagging voice told her it was her own fault for telling Sophie she had to come in.

After making herself a cup of tea, Meredith went back to bed. Within minutes she was falling asleep again, the tea the least of her priorities

Chapter Twelve

9 December

Stanley buttoned his shirt and put on his tie, then realised he was humming a tune he used to sing to Edie. 'We'll Meet Again' by Vera Lynn seemed appropriate, and for the first time it made him happy not sad. He made himself a pot of tea, setting out, as usual, a cup for Edie too, and buttered himself a slice of toast. Yes, he was feeling very positive. What a difference meeting new people could make.

She really would have to go to see a doctor soon, thought Meredith. This wasn't normal, but first she needed to go through the schedule, check how the salespeople were performing against target for the month and set in place any corrective action plans. After about the thirteenth of December everyone would be in holiday mode, both staff and clients alike, and not much would be achieved. At least Sophie was back now.

A few hours into her day Meredith decided she had to get out of the office. She'd nip over to Sugar and Spice for a slice of that gorgeous caramel shortcake. Maybe they'd even have some Christmas drinks. What she wouldn't give for a warming Glühwein right now, although she guessed they wouldn't have an alcohol licence. Well, perhaps they would have a cinnamon latte. Meredith stopped short. She didn't usually buy into all this Christmas claptrap, but right now, the thought of it was quite soothing.

'Hi there, nice to see you again,' the woman greeted Meredith warmly, as she entered the bakery. The smell of fresh pastries and just brewed coffee assailed her senses and Meredith breathed in deeply, before another coughing fit racked her body.

'Oh dear, that sounds awful. You should get that seen to,' the woman offered.

Thanks, Einstein, thought Meredith uncharitably. She gave the woman a tight smile, then said, 'Do you have any Glühwein?'

'I'm afraid we don't have a licence.'

'Right. I see. Well, do you have any Christmas drinks, any specialties?'

'We do have a cinnamon drink and also a cranberry tea, and I've made cranberry and white chocolate muffins in honour of the season,' the woman said.

'Yes, cranberry tea sounds good. Cranberry's good for you when you're not feeling great, isn't it?' Meredith said.

'That's right; cranberries are high in antioxidants.'

'Well, in that case, I'll have cranberry tea and the muffin, thanks. In fact, can you make that two muffins? Sophie will probably want one, too, although I don't know whether she likes them or not,' Meredith thought out loud.

Just then another fit of coughing came over Meredith. She withdrew a handkerchief from her coat pocket and coughed violently into it. But she didn't stop. She kept coughing and coughing and then started wheezing and turned blue. The bakery patrons looked on in horror. She couldn't seem to get a breath.

'Let's sit you down, my dear,' the woman said, but

just as she was coming around the counter to help her, Meredith's legs gave way and she collapsed. A man sitting close by jumped up to try to catch her, but didn't quite get there in time and Meredith fell, her head grazing a chair on the way down.

'Jacob, get some water, please,' Natalie called. 'Stand back, please,' she said to the customers, 'I'm a first-aider.'

The shocked customers cleared a space around Meredith.

'She's awfully pale,' one of them remarked.

Natalie checked Meredith's airway wasn't blocked. Her breathing was still raspy, but at least she *was* breathing. Her pulse was faint.

'Jacob, call an ambulance,' Natalie said, as she moved Meredith into the recovery position.

Jacob rushed around the counter and dialled 999.

The paramedics arrived within ten minutes. There was no change to Meredith's condition; she was still unconscious. Whilst they were waiting for the ambulance, Natalie had kept an eye on her, but also asked if anyone knew where she worked. No-one in the café knew her and unfortunately they had no way of contacting Sophie. After a few minutes Natalie had the brainwave of checking for an ICE in her phone; hopefully she would have her emergency contact listed. Jacob searched through her bag, until he found an iPhone. Unfortunately it was locked and they had no way of knowing the password. Then Jacob came across a business card wallet. Withdrawing a card, he read *Meredith Storm, Storm Communications*. He dialled the number on the card and asked for Sophie.

As the paramedics put Meredith into the ambulance with the café clientele watching them and Natalie filling them in on what had happened, an out-of-breath Sophie appeared from round the corner.

'Oh God, what happened?'

'Are you her daughter?' the paramedic asked.

'No, she doesn't have any children. I'm her assistant. Can I come with her?'

'I suppose that would be all right. Get in.'

The ambulance set off with its siren blaring. Sophie's mind was racing. She'd have to contact Amelia, Meredith's sister. But first she needed to find out what had happened. She talked with the paramedic as the ambulance rushed to Vale of Leven hospital and he relayed what Natalie had told him. Sophie remembered that Meredith had been paler than her usual self and had been coughing a great deal that morning, but then Sophie hadn't thought much of it – she herself had been ill this week, with no sympathy from Meredith.

Stanley's second visit to the club went even better than the first. Now that he had registered, the centre sent a bus to pick him up around ten in the morning, which suited him, particularly in this bad weather, as he was nervous about relying on his stick to keep his balance.

Angus and George greeted Stanley when he arrived and he chatted with them for a few minutes before heading over to the reading corner. He had noticed it on Friday, but hadn't had time to sift through the books. It would save him going to the library if there was anything he fancied.

Ten minutes later, he was seated in a comfy chair, talking to a woman about seaside resorts of yesteryear and the beauty of the Hebrides, a book by Clive Cussler in his lap.

'Would you two like a cup of tea?' Cathy's assistant, Betty, asked the pair.

They both nodded and resumed their conversation. Within a few minutes they had a cup of tea each and a plate of chocolate and plain biscuits beside them to share.

'Right, everyone. I'm going to hand you out some newspapers and I'd like you to have a wee read, and in half an hour we're going to have a little discussion on today's headlines,' said Cathy, as she distributed newspapers to each table.

'That sounds like fun,' said Stanley. 'A bit like a debating society.'

'I like it,' Ruth, the lady he was chatting to said. 'We do this every Monday morning, as we get all the news from the weekend, too.'

They picked up the newspapers and began leafing through them, oohing and aahing at some of the stories.

'Oh, I can't believe he died! He was one of my favourites,' Ruth said.

'Who's that?' Stanley asked, interested.

'John Rainier, the actor. He was in that film with Audrey Hepburn. What was the name again?'

Stanley admitted he didn't know the film, although he knew the actor.

'He must have been a good age,' Stanley said.

'In his nineties, I think,' said Ruth, scanning the article to see if it told her. 'Yes, here it is, ninety-five.'

'He had a good innings.' Stanley thought then of his only son, who had died before his time, abroad, killed in a skiing accident.

'Right, we better get back to these headlines, or we'll look like a right pair of dummies,' said Ruth, touching him lightly on the arm.

Stanley felt the warmth of her fingers. He hadn't been touched by another human being since Edie's funeral, except when people bumped into him by accident on the street. That simple action of warmth and camaraderie made him feel human, whole again.

As she sat in the pub overlooking Loch Lomond, next to the burning log fire, Rebecca was struck by the irony. Trust Ethan to choose a romantic location when they were dividing up their personal possessions. The man had no empathy whatsoever, no clue. She zoned out temporarily as he ran through the list he had prepared of things which were clearly his and items which they had bought together but which he thought he was entitled to, and outlined his reasons why.

How can he be so insensitive? How can it be reduced to this? How can I have spent three years of my life with this man?

When Rebecca had first entered the pub, late as usual, Ethan had been sitting near the fire warming his hands, his jacket still on. She had stood in the doorway watching him and her heart had missed a beat. How was she going to get over him? She fought back the desire to burst into tears and, closing the door behind her, walked up to the sofa where he was sitting.

'Hello, Ethan,' she'd said. There had been little preamble after the 'pleasantries' of asking how they each were and, in her case, lying about how she really was. *Set adrift, tearful, abandoned* probably weren't the words he wanted to hear, so she said, 'I'm fine. Getting on with things, you know.'

'So, are you looking forward to Christmas?' he'd asked.

'Not exactly.' She stared at him. *What a moron!*

'Right, no, I don't suppose you are.' He'd had the good grace to study his shoes at that point.

Now as he inventoried the things he wanted to keep from the flat, leaving Rebecca with virtually nothing and trying to make it sound as if she was getting a good deal, Rebecca couldn't help but loathe him. *How dare he? Does he think I'm totally stupid?*

Ethan must have thought she'd be so resigned to the end of their relationship she'd just roll over and say, *'Yes, Ethan, no Ethan, three bags full, Ethan,'* but he didn't know her as well as he thought. From somewhere deep inside came a resolve not to be trodden all over.

'And I'll need your keys soon, as it wouldn't really be right, you having access to the flat, when it's no longer yours.'

'You'll get the keys, Ethan, once everything's sorted out, and no, I don't agree that you should keep the wardrobe, or the washing machine, or the bookcases. Can you tell me exactly what you think I should have of our joint purchases, as it seems to me that you don't think I should have anything much at all.'

Ethan shrank back. Rebecca had never talked to him like that before; few people did. No, this was a change from her usual compliant self. His dumbstruck reaction amused her; he actually took a few seconds to recover.

'Well…well, I suppose you could keep a few other items,' he finally managed to blurt out.

'A few other items.' Rebecca was incensed. 'What items have you already proposed I keep?' she said matter-of-factly, folding her arms to clarify she meant business.

'Well…' began Ethan '…I was thinking…what about the microwave and the blender?'

'Really?' Rebecca's sarcasm was plain. 'So we bought a houseful of furniture together, you made me sell my fridge freezer, bed and a few other things, for which I got a pittance, and you think I should get items with a combined value of a hundred quid? Well, you can think again.'

Taking advantage of the fact that Ethan appeared staggered by this resourceful, belligerent Rebecca, she said, 'I want the washing machine, wardrobe, bookcases and that's just to make up for you making me sell my stuff. Remember, you're the one who wanted to end this, so you can hardly expect to get all the spoils, too.'

In the face of this new Rebecca, Ethan backed down. They ran through his list again, with Rebecca being fair, but ensuring she had what she was entitled to.

'My lawyer will be in touch with yours about buying you out,' Ethan said as they wound things up.

'Well, I hope you're happy. I'm glad you split up with me, because you've revealed your true colours.' Rebecca swung her coat over her shoulders, picked up her bag and left, but not before she saw Ethan standing with his jaw almost reaching the floor.

Chapter Thirteen

10 December

As Natalie walked to work that morning, she was inspired by the number of Christmas tree lights she saw in the houses she passed. Several people had decorated the trees outside their homes, whether they were Christmas trees or not, so strings of white lights could be found hanging from ash, beech and elm trees, as well as the expected firs. It made Natalie's heart soar to see the spirit of the season embraced in this way. Everyone was happier at Christmas, well, not everyone, but generally speaking, people showed more goodwill towards their fellow men and women.

On the way back from work yesterday she'd stopped in at the garden centre and ordered a small Christmas tree to be delivered to the bakery the following day. So she carried a large bag containing Christmas lights, an angel, and lastly, an assortment of baubles from all over the world. Some were handmade or bespoke, others were valuable, such as the snowflake with twenty-six diamonds inlaid and two ruby-encrusted rings circling it, whilst others had sentimental value; the paper angel her great-niece had made for her, a fine example. Natalie had been collecting baubles all her life; some people collected stamps, others Pokemon figures or football stickers, she collected Christmas decorations.

Natalie spent the early part of the morning mixing and tasting, measuring ingredients and refining flavours. She was also working on her latest Christmas cake of the day – *Tronco de Navidad* – a firm Spanish favourite. It kind of resembled a yule log – layers of creamy mousse with a thick chocolate frosting. Grooves made it resemble the bark of a tree, and mushrooms, raspberries, and holly leaves all made of marzipan adorned it. Natalie had thought it particularly fitting for today, as the Yule log placed in the hearth was supposed to burn for the twelve days of Christmas, and here they were, twelve days before Christmas, by European standards if not by British. She'd always preferred the European custom of making Christmas Eve the big occasion, unlike the British way of only celebrating on the twenty-fifth. It was probably because she wasn't much good at containing her excitement.

Jacob hadn't been so happy in a long time. Having a job to go to every day, even if it was only working in a bakery, gave him a sense of purpose and belonging. To someone who had often felt unwelcome in his own home, as if he were somehow a nuisance, spending time in this busy but relaxed bakery was balm to his soul. Natalie was a great boss to work for: really kind, a genuinely good person, plus he was getting to know the locals as he had never done in the past. He was amazed at how interesting he found old people, and he didn't mean people in their fifties, but those in their late sixties and above. In retrospect, he supposed he should have considered them more exciting in the past – they'd been around a long time, but it simply had never occurred to him that they would have anything in common. He'd heard stories from friends who had grandparents, of being bored rigid by tales of the war, but he discovered that they didn't only talk about the war, but politics, too, in which he was very interested. They discussed old movies, from well before his time, but which he enjoyed, with screen greats like Clark Gable, Rita Hayworth and James Stewart. They spoke of how travel had been difficult, life before the internet, before cars were commonplace, before TV, for goodness' sake. Jacob couldn't imagine life without any of these things, so he lapped up their stories.

Every time the door opened, Jacob wondered if it would be Rebecca. It had been a few days since her last visit and he hoped he hadn't seen the last of her.

At twelve thirty, Sophie entered the bakery, panting, cheeks ruddy with cold, her blonde hair piled on top of her head.

'Hi.' She spoke first to Natalie, who had walked towards her. 'I just wanted to thank you both for the other day. And I thought you might want to know how Meredith was doing. Sorry I haven't been in before, it's been a bit manic.' She unwound her scarf and draped it and her coat over a nearby chair.

'No need to apologise, my dear,' Natalie told her. 'So how is she?'

'She's stable, although still in hospital. She has pneumonia.'

'Pneumonia, eh? That is serious.' Natalie shook her head. 'Poor woman.'

'Yes, well, the doctors have said she might be able to get out by the end of the week, as long as she has someone to care for her at home. But she lives alone, so her sister has offered to put her up.'

'That's what families are for. She's lucky to have such an accommodating family.'

'You're not kidding. Amelia's great, but she has four kids. I don't know how she'll manage, but she's assured the doctors she will.'

'Well, I'm glad to hear she's getting better. And what about you, are you taking care of yourself?' Natalie asked.

Sophie was touched. No-one ever asked her how she was doing. They just assumed she would get on with it. Tears welled up in her eyes, and she bit her lip to prevent herself from crying. The truth was she felt stressed-out, which was why she had come to the bakery to sit in and have a latte and a piece of cake, before returning to the madhouse which was a dynamic company without its CEO at the helm, with no-one except Sophie to assume responsibility, even though she was only a lowly assistant. Meredith had been so intent on not trusting anyone to do anything, she hadn't allowed for the eventuality that one day she might not be in a position to manage everything herself.

Although Sophie was rising to the challenge, she had all but slept at the office the past few days. She'd also been at the hospital twice to see how Meredith was doing; pale and a lesser version of herself, pitiful, were the words which came to mind. Always so strong and, well, scary, Meredith in a position of weakness didn't compute.

'I'm surviving, just,' Sophie replied. 'Thanks for asking. It hasn't been easy and I daresay it'll get worse before it gets better, but I'll manage somehow.' Returning to the other reason she was here, Sophie asked if she could have a slice of the Cake of the Day and a latte. 'I'm going to sit in today.'

'Quite right, too. You need a little break,' agreed Natalie. 'Jacob will bring your order over shortly.'

Jacob, who had been standing beside Natalie, and had

overheard the conversation, but had been serving other customers, smiled warmly at Sophie. 'I like the way you've done your hair today.'

Sophie blushed. 'Oh this? It's just the quickest thing in the morning. Takes five seconds.'

Since he had no great plans today, and the weather was miserable, Stanley decided he would go through his photo albums. He'd never got around to cataloguing many of them properly, so today he was going to sort them out. He'd make himself a nice cup of tea first and read a bit of his book. He was finding it a bit more hard-going than some of the author's previous books, as it was technology-related, a subject about which Stanley knew little.

Just then the letterbox rattled and a thud heralded the arrival of the morning's mail. Stanley shuffled off to retrieve it. His arthritis was getting worse, he noticed, as he sat at the table and opened the letters with difficulty. Quarterly gas bill. He hadn't received his winter fuel payment yet. He gasped when he saw the total. Could it really be that much? He was always so careful and only ever had one radiator on in the house.

Sighing, Stanley decided he'd have to economise more for the next few months, both on fuel and on other essentials. He wondered if he was eligible for any other benefits. You always heard on TV of millions of pounds in unclaimed benefits because few people knew they were entitled to them. Perhaps it was worth a trip to the Department of Work and Pensions to find out. He couldn't phone them as he couldn't hear very well on the phone, even with his two hearing aids and the special phone with hearing assistance. Then there were all those confusing menus to get through. Why couldn't a real person just answer the phone on the other end? And they were always in such a hurry to get you off the phone.

Setting the bill aside for a moment, Stanley picked up the remaining letters. A Christmas card, with a gold bauble on the front and a frosted finish. Glitter came away on his hands; a lovely card.

To Stanley from John and Maureen, Merry Christmas. A lump formed in Stanley's throat. That's how it would be from now on. To Stanley; not to Stanley and Edie, or Edie and Stanley, but Stanley – just Stanley – alone. Stanley wiped away a tear which had come unbidden to his eye. *Oh Edie, my darling, how I miss you.* He turned his attention to the last letter and on opening it was met with a robin perched on a gate, snow all around him, a cottage featuring a roaring log fire in the background. *To Edie and Stanley, Love at Christmas, Elizabeth and Robert.*

Stanley couldn't work out what was worse, for Edie to have been eradicated altogether from the previous card and her absence made all the more notable, or for someone not to have been informed of his wife's passing. Elizabeth and Robert, from Calgary, friends of friends. He would have to find their address and write to them, send them a card, but also somehow mention the fact that Edie was no longer with them, save them getting it wrong next year. Possibly they would be embarrassed, but best to set the record straight and hopefully Stanley wouldn't receive a card next year still addressed to his much-loved but now departed wife.

It had felt liberating to be so strong for a change when confronted with Ethan. A sense of pride had swept over Rebecca at standing up for herself, although when she had reached her car the night before, her legs were shaking and she was glad to be able to drop into the driver's seat before they gave way. This new sense of empowerment was short-lived, however, as the harsh reality that was spending Christmas without a partner reared its head again.

Everywhere she looked there was Christmas. Every second house now had its Christmas lights on. For her part, buying a Christmas tree was the furthest thing from her mind. She and Ethan had always done that as a couple, a key part of the Christmas proceedings. They even decorated it together. He was the only man she knew who wasn't a parent, who enjoyed such things. How could their relationship change so quickly? She still didn't know what had gone wrong. What was clear to her now, though, was that they weren't meant for each other. The coldness he had displayed towards her the night before, the fact that he could instil such anger in her, usually such a placid person, told her that.

But it didn't make spending Christmas without a boyfriend any more palatable. There were parties to go to, relatives to field questions from about the breakup, new arrangements to make for Christmas Day. Hannah had already said she could spend Christmas with her and Rebecca would have preferred to, but her mother had insisted she come to them. She would be pitied and fussed over, loved really, but sometimes you just needed space. She could have had that with Hannah, both of them single and in similar circumstances, well, sort of, Hannah hadn't just been dumped. Instead she'd have to endure twenty questions from her mother, who was a big Ethan fan, although ultimately her loyalties lay with her daughter, or so Rebecca hoped.

As she walked through the supermarket, Rebecca tried to avoid any Christmas-related areas, but even the wine aisle had seasonal offers. Items on her shopping list weren't in their usual place, as products had been rejigged to accommodate all the Christmas stock. Where she'd usually find the gravy granules was now home to selection boxes and tins of Quality Street and Roses; the latter one of the key reasons half the country had to diet in January, with office staff gorging themselves throughout December on chocolate from well-meaning bosses and clients.

She had fancied grilled halloumi for dinner, but was having difficulty finding the Cypriot cheese amongst the array of *selected specially for Christmas* cheese boards and other cheese gifts. Since she was here, maybe she could get one of those for Christmas Day, her way of contributing to the Christmas meal. Her mother would never accept money from her and would be horrified if she offered. Their home was still her home, even though she hadn't lived in it for five years.

The cosmetics aisle played host to a giddy assortment of bath sets and bubble baths, body scrubs and bath crèmes, in brightly coloured packaging, festooned with ribbons and lace. All Rebecca wanted was a bottle of moisturiser, but she was foiled once again. Where had they put the damned moisturisers?

And to cap it all off, the supermarket was playing Wizzard's 'I Wish It Could Be Christmas Everyday'. Even that couldn't lift her spirits. Rebecca wasn't looking forward to Christmas this year, not one bit.

Chapter Fourteen

11 December

The more clement weather meant that those who had stayed tucked up indoors now ventured out. A light drizzle was still falling but the snow had melted, leaving behind only clumps of brown slush here and there. The relief of it being once again above zero degrees was almost palpable.

As a result the bakery was swamped. Both Jacob and Natalie had been rushed off their feet all morning. Since she checked the forecast every night, Natalie had anticipated they might be busier and had come in even earlier that morning to start whipping up her creations. They'd already sold out of that day's Christmas special – mouth-watering cupcakes emblazoned with tiny Christmas trees, robins, presents and carol singers. Jacob had remarked wryly that they were going like hot cakes. Natalie had groaned at him. She put batch after batch in the oven, but still she couldn't keep up. Eventually she decided not to try, as she wanted to ensure they could sell the rest of the day's stock. She would make more the next day.

The Christmas tree, which she had expected to be delivered yesterday, arrived only today, amid much apologising by the garden centre. A mix-up with labels had meant it had been sent to someone else before they noticed their mistake. They would give it to her for half price because of the inconvenience. Natalie accepted and thanked them. She would get around to putting it up later.

Things calmed down a little around three o'clock, and Jacob and Natalie decided to take a break.

'Let's have a cup of tea before we do anything else,' Natalie suggested. 'I'm going to dress the tree shortly. Do you want to help?'

'Sure.'

Natalie untangled the lights they'd found. 'I'll sort the lights, you choose the baubles.'

'I don't really know much about dressing a tree, but I'll do what I can,' Jacob said, although really he meant he would put the fairy or angel or star at the top. He didn't really expect Natalie to need his opinion on much else, but Natalie had other ideas.

'I think this is the best spot, don't you?'

'Hmm,' Jacob said, non-committally.

'Right, have a rummage through those baubles there and take out five you like.'

'I'm not really a bauble kind of person. I don't know anything about them.'

'Trust me, everyone's a bauble person. Go on, what have you got to lose?'

Reluctantly Jacob delved into the bag and discovered that it was full of lots of individual boxes. He took one out; it looked very unusual, then he saw it was made of wood. Opening it, he pulled out a glass heart; it was pretty heavy. 'This is really nice. He turned to Natalie, weighing it in his hand.

'Ah, the Kiev heart. Did you know that Ukrainians celebrate Christmas on the seventh of January, but they

90

decorate their Christmas trees on the sixth?'

Admitting his ignorance on the subject, Jacob stuck his hand into the bag once more. Another box, this time a miniature glass Christmas tree, and so it went on, with Natalie explaining the history behind each one.

Jacob had shown a genuine interest in decorating the tree when it became clear that Natalie viewed doing so with such reverence and had gone to painstaking lengths to ensure that the tree was spectacular. And all this just for a tree for the bakery. Jacob wavered between mystified and impressed.

Just as he passed the last bauble to Natalie, his mobile rang. 'Just a sec,' he said, heading through the back to take his phone out of his winter jacket. The screen flashed at him as he picked it up. *Tabitha.*

'Hey, sis, how you doing?' Hearing his sister's voice always cheered him.

He listened to her and then said, 'Really? Of course you can come for Christmas. Stay as long as you want. I can't believe it!'

Tabitha continued to give him details, and it transpired that she wanted to come the following day. Jacob was delighted.

'Everything OK?' Natalie asked when he returned to the task of decorating the tree.

'More than OK.' Jacob grinned. 'My sister's coming for Christmas. Actually, she's coming tomorrow and staying right through Christmas.'

'Oh, that's wonderful. I'm not surprised you look like the cat who got the cream.' Natalie smiled at him. 'There, what do you think of the tree?'

Jacob stood back and admired it: the amazing baubles, no tinsel and the white fairy lights; it glowed in an almost otherworldly fashion. What was he like? His good news had made him go soft in the head. 'It looks fantastic, very Christmassy.'

'Perfect, exactly the desired effect. The garden centre had them at such a good price and the trees there really are lovely, not the sad specimens some of these cowboys try to pass off at full price and which barely last until Christmas.'

Jacob nodded his agreement. Yes, he'd seen some scrawny Christmas trees come Christmas Day, too. Perhaps that's why some people only bought theirs the week before Christmas.

As they closed up the bakery and said goodnight, Jacob walked home happier than he had felt in a long time. Maybe Christmas wouldn't be so bad after all.

On the other side of town, Stanley had had a great day, his third at the club. Not only had he made some new friends, both male and female, but he liked the ambiance, the staff and the camaraderie. He looked forward to the days when he went to the club, and knowing he had a busier schedule meant he felt more content being at home, pottering around, doing the occasional bits and pieces of housework, or watching telly, on the days he wasn't there.

He hadn't been into the bakery for a few days. He'd need to go and try some of their Christmas cakes. Word was that the new woman, Natalie, was doing a different Christmas cake every day; so one of his cronies at the club had told him.

Today he'd played dominoes and won, a first for him in a long time. Edie hadn't much liked playing dominoes. Lunch had been good, too: pea and ham soup followed by chicken and bacon parcels with roast potatoes, gravy and baby carrots. At this time of year and especially when the temperatures were so low, having a hot meal prepared for him made all the difference. He'd never had to think about it before; Edie had done all the cooking. Oh, how he missed her. He talked to her over their cups of tea, telling her all about the new people he was meeting and how she would have liked them. He'd enjoyed a lively debate about the latest news items, and the members of the club had been divided over certain issues. But there was no hostility – it was all in good fun and everyone seemed nice and relaxed. He was glad to have found the club and could no longer imagine how he had got through the days before going there.

There had been much talk of Christmas, and Cathy and a few other women who ran the club had been decorating the rooms for them whilst the members ate lunch. Stanley wouldn't be getting a tree this year. What was the point? Who would see it? And what was he going to do, put a present to himself under it? No, far better not to have the hassle when there was only himself to think about. His gifts from his grandson usually arrived sometime between Christmas and New Year, occasionally even after New Year, depending on the postal services. Christmas was the worst time of year to send gifts abroad. They took an age to reach the recipient, arrived damaged or not at all. He would have to start thinking about his grandson's gift. Edie dealt with all of that, usually. He had no idea what to buy. He had heard someone mention last postal dates, though, and he had the impression that he had missed it. Oh well, like everything else, the gifts would arrive late. He really must put some thought into what Thomas would like.

The high point of the day, though, was that he had been invited to the pub the following night. The pub! He hadn't been to a pub in about fifteen years. Edie wasn't much of a drinker and he'd either lost touch with his drinking buddies or they had died. When you got to his age, he thought, it really was that simple. So, he was looking forward to going to Corrigans the following evening, with a few of his new pals from the club. What did you wear to the pub these days? he wondered. Would a dress jacket over a shirt and tie be too formal? That's what he liked to wear normally when he went out. Decisions, decisions.

Chapter Fifteen

12 December

The bakery and café had been chock-a-block since they opened their doors. The first customers commented on the beautiful tree with its highly original decorations. A young mother had to stop her toddler from dismantling it, whilst a sheepish-looking young man just managed to stop his dog weeing on it. Customers continued to ask how Mrs Williams' recovery was going, and for Natalie to pass on their regards to her. 'What a time of year to be laid up,' they said. 'Poor thing.' Natalie had gone over the books again the night before and felt pleased that the owner could hardly fail to be happy with the takings since her arrival. And so far she didn't seem to have lost her any customers…on the contrary.

It was difficult to say whether the tree was the hot discussion topic of the day, or that day's Christmas cake special – *torta negra de Navidad* – a traditional Venezuelan Christmas cake, which didn't originate in Venezuela, Natalie told those who asked about the recipe.

Rushed off his feet all morning, Jacob didn't notice Rebecca come in. She had gone to lay her coat and hat over a vacant chair, since there were few left. As she turned to come back to the counter, he shot her a huge smile. He was elated to see her and thought she looked even more beautiful than last time, despite her hair being a little mussed from the wind outside; her flushed cheeks only adding to her attractiveness. She was like a goddess, but seemed oblivious to how pretty she was. Fortunately he had stopped becoming tongue-tied when she was around. He made some small talk with her as he took her order, then told her he would bring it over.

As Natalie cleared the tables, she also picked up the newspapers which were lying on various tables and put them back on their rack; all but one. Just then the bell tinkled, indicating someone entering the bakery. Sophie breezed in, a gust of wind closing the door behind her. Gathering the crockery and plates containing only a few cake crumbs – just what she liked to see – Natalie headed towards the counter.

'Good afternoon, Sophie. How are you?'

'I'm good, thanks. You? Busy?'

'Oh yes, this is it quiet.' She indicated the still full bakery café. 'And how's your boss?'

'Getting better, although she needs to take it easy. All going well she might be out tomorrow,' Sophie said, as she tugged at a loose thread on her coat, glancing every now and then to her left.

Natalie followed her gaze and saw Jacob chatting to Rebecca, handing her a hot chocolate and a piece of Christmas cake.

'That's good,' she said, thoughts whirring around inside her head. 'So, are you staying for a bit today, or do you need to rush back?'

After sneaking a peek at table two, Sophie said, 'No,

I have to get back. Things are pretty hectic. I'm barely keeping everything afloat. It's just as well I'm so organised and in tune with Meredith's ways and appointments, or we really would be in trouble. Maybe tomorrow.'

'No problem. What are you having then?'

Sophie opted for Natalie's recommendation of the Cake of the Day and a skinny latte. As Sophie left the bakery, Natalie smiled to herself. *All in good time.*

Jacob returned to the counter and left Rebecca in peace to drink her hot chocolate.

'You missed Sophie. She came in to update us on Meredith and get some things to take away.'

'Really?' Jacob's face fell. 'How's she doing?'

'Sophie or Meredith?' Natalie asked, trying not to smirk.

'Erm, both,' said Jacob, blinking rapidly.

The corners of Natalie's mouth twitched as she said, 'All going well, Meredith will be out tomorrow, and Sophie's frazzled, poor dear. She could do with a good night out, I think.'

'Yes, she does have a lot on her plate,' Jacob agreed, as he stacked the dishwasher and wiped the counter with a cloth.

The newspaper which had been left on the table wasn't one Rebecca would usually read, but she'd gone into her bag to take out her e-reader and then realised she had left it charging at home. *Damn!* Oh well, at least she could read the paper. She took a tentative sip of her hot chocolate, as steam was still rising from it. *Mmm – lovely.*

She leafed through the usual tales of backstabbing politicians, policies various parties were at odds over, and skipped over who was blowing up who this week. She also flipped past the celebrity gossip pages and headed straight for an article about how Royal Mail shares were doing. She nibbled at her cake every now and then, enjoying a bit of quiet time, although the scene around her was a frenzied one, with frantic shoppers popping into the bakery for a sit-down and a rest, after hours of trawling the shops, before getting back to it.

As Rebecca turned the page, the first thing she noticed was *The Melbourne Gallery – Assistant Manager – wanted for immediate start. Closing date 20 December*. She read the full job description, her heart beating faster with every word. This was her dream job. This was what she'd been waiting for; these kinds of jobs never came up, or seldom. The salary band was rare, although it did say dependent on experience, but she had the experience. She couldn't pass up the chance. She loved working for her boss, but she needed to be challenged more, never mind that the extra cash would come in handy. Taking a pen from her bag, Rebecca noted down the number and made a brief note of the details.

With a sense of mounting excitement, Rebecca downed her hot chocolate and finished the remainder of her cake. Grabbing her bag, and with her mobile in her hand, Rebecca waved goodbye to Natalie and Jacob and set off at a brisk pace down the street. She didn't want everyone knowing her business and she had to make this call now before she talked herself out of it. She identified a quiet side street, where there were no carol singers belting out 'Silent Night', and dialled the number she had written down.

'The Melbourne Gallery, how may I help you?' a polite, well-educated voice said.

'Good afternoon.' Rebecca tried for equally polite, dispensing with her habitual 'hi'. 'May I speak with

Dominic Melbourne, please?'

'May I ask what it's in connection with?'

'Yes. It's regarding the advert in *The Scotsman*.'

'I see, let me see if he's available.'

Rebecca thanked the girl, then hung on as she was subjected to yet another rendition of Handel's Water Music. Why didn't firms vary their hold music more? she wondered. She had begun to loathe that particular piece of music after having to endure it when on hold to the bank, her insurance company, even her hairdresser.

'Dominic Melbourne speaking,' a deep, sexy voice said down the line.

'Good afternoon, Mr Melbourne. My name's Rebecca Cowan. I saw your advert for Assistant Manager in *The Scotsman*. I'm very interested in the role and was wondering if you'd consider me for the post.'

'Well, I'll need your CV, first of all, but why don't we do a little on-the-spot interview now?' Mr Melbourne said.

Now? thought Rebecca. *Now!* Jeez – she wasn't ready. *Right, c'mon, you can do this*, she told herself, mentally giving herself a shake.

'That would be great,' she said, more confidently than she felt. Exuding self-assurance would be crucial to being chosen for the role.

Dominic Melbourne then proceeded to grill Rebecca on certain aspects of her work history, her current position, her knowledge of the art world, and her contacts, before finally declaring twenty minutes later, 'OK, I'm happy enough to consider you as a candidate. How's Monday for you?'

Monday would be her first day back at work after her week-long holiday, but Rebecca had a good feeling about this job, so she said Monday was fine. They agreed a time and Dominic told her to speak to his receptionist for directions, should she need any. When she came off the phone, Rebecca clapped her hands together in glee.

Finally, a possibility to advance her career. She'd certainly waited long enough. But what should she wear? To her knowledge, she had nothing art gallery assistant manager-ish in her wardrobe. Still, it would give her and Hannah a good excuse to go shopping on Saturday – not that they ever needed an excuse and even less so at Christmas, well most Christmases. With an unmistakable spring in her step, Rebecca bounced along to her next port of call – the pub – it wasn't every day you secured an interview for your dream job.

Chapter Sixteen

13 December

There were only two of them this year, thank goodness – Friday the thirteenths, that is. Natalie always felt she had to work a little bit harder on those days, particularly if they fell in December. There was always the possibility that Fate or other forces might be working against her. If she'd known of Jacob's plans, she would have tried to prevent him from carrying them out, would have subtly hinted that another day might have suited better.

Rebecca had come into the café mid-morning and hugged both her and Jacob. She wasn't surprised, though, when Jacob turned an interesting shade of red. Almost pillar box.

'What's all this about?' Natalie asked her.

'You know how I was in yesterday?' Rebecca beamed at her.

'Yes.' Natalie recollected her being there when she had been talking to Sophie.

'Well, if it hadn't been for you–' Rebecca's eyes shone as she looked first at Natalie then Jacob '–I wouldn't have an interview as assistant manager of The Melbourne Gallery.'

'What's that?' asked Jacob, confused. Natalie noticed

that although he didn't seem to be following Rebecca's reasoning, he seemed delighted she was hugging them.

'Sorry, I'm getting ahead of myself. Yesterday when I was here, *The Scotsman* was lying on the table.'

'Right,' said Jacob, shrugging.

'Well, after reading through loads of the articles, I came across a job advert. I took the number, called them up and they did a telephone interview. I've to go for a face-to-face interview on Monday.' Rebecca jiggled on the spot, her excitement obvious.

'That's brilliant,' said Jacob. 'Really good news. Congratulations.'

'Well, I haven't had the interview yet, but you know how difficult it is to even get an interview at the moment.'

Rebecca had no way of knowing just how much Jacob knew that feeling. On his second day he had told Natalie his tale of woe, how he had had more than his fair share of rejection letters, and worse, no word at all from around ninety-five percent of applications. That was the hardest thing – not even hearing back, but then he knew there could be between twenty and two hundred people going after one job.

'This calls for a celebratory hot chocolate,' said Natalie, 'And today's Christmas cake, if you fancy it?'

'Oh, yes please. What's today's cake?'

'Today I've made *cozonac romanesc*, it's a Romanian Christmas cake, a bit like the Italian *panettone*.'

'Sounds wonderful and light; probably doesn't even count as eating cake from a calorie point of view, right?' Rebecca winked at Natalie.

'Absolutely not!' came the reply of her partner in crime.

'Pity we don't have an alcohol licence, or we could toast you,' said Jacob.

'Oh, don't worry, I stopped in at the pub for a glass of wine after I called them. Well, if you're going to celebrate, do it in style, right?' Rebecca shot him a huge grin, which reduced him to a deep crimson.

'Right, why don't you go and sit yourself down and Jacob will bring your things over?' Natalie said, as one of the suppliers arrived just then, asking her to check and sign for some goods.

'Can you bring it round the back, please?' Natalie asked. 'Jacob, I won't be long. Can you manage?'

'Sure, I'll just get Rebecca her order.'

Whilst Natalie attended to the deliveries, Jacob whistled along to the radio as he prepared Rebecca's hot chocolate. Nat King Cole's 'When I Fall In Love' came on next. Jacob plated up Rebecca's cake and took it towards her on a tray, still whistling.

Rebecca smiled up at him, amused, as he placed the items on the table. Emboldened by her expression, Jacob decided it was now or never.

'Rebecca?'

'Yes?'

'Can I ask you something?'

'Sure. Today's probably the best day. I feel like a kid in a sweetshop,' she said.

Hoping he would feel the same after asking his question, Jacob said, 'I just wondered if you might like to go for dinner or see a film one night?'

Rebecca stared at him and Jacob knew he had said the wrong thing. What an idiot. What had he done wrong? Was it the way he had phrased it?

Then Rebecca gave a wry smile and said, 'Jacob, you're a really nice guy, and if the timing had been different, perhaps I would have taken you up on your offer, but I'm literally in the middle of a bad breakup,' Rebecca confided in him. 'I'm at the stage of deciding who gets which items of furniture and you're too nice to be my rebound guy,' she said sadly.

'It's fine. Forget I asked.'

'No, I'm flattered you did – thank you.'

'No, seriously, please, forget I asked. I don't want things to be awkward when you're here.'

'They won't be,' Rebecca reassured him.

How embarrassing. The worst of it was he would gladly have been anything to her, rebound guy included. He appreciated that Rebecca wasn't in a position to start a new relationship, but it still didn't buoy his spirits. Jacob retreated behind the counter with his joie de vivre somewhat muted.

Natalie didn't ask what was wrong with him, but she worked it out from the glances he gave Rebecca and those she threw him. Sighing, she thought, *My job isn't always easy.*

It was with a heavy heart and a broken one that Jacob headed home that night, but he perked up when he remembered his sister would be there. She'd arrived the night before. They'd stayed up late drinking, well, he had. Tabitha said she was too tired and anyway it was red wine he had in, which always gave her shocking hangovers.

'Hello, darling brother.' Tabitha hugged him around his middle as he came into the hall.

'What do you want?' he said flatly.

'Hey!' Tabitha grabbed Jacob by the arm and turned him to face her. 'What's up?'

'Nothing.'

'Jacob, spill, now!'

Reluctantly he told her about his conversation with Rebecca.

'OK, that's pretty crappy, but it's not as if she told you to bog off or anything. She's only just split up with this guy and the last thing you want to do is get involved with someone who's still caught up in another relationship.'

Jacob admitted the truth of this, then said, 'Mmm, what's that smell?'

'That,' said Tabitha, turning towards the kitchen, 'is my aubergine cannelloni.'

'Smells better than it sounds,' grumbled Jacob. 'Where's the meat?'

'Oh shush, you'll love it, I guarantee you.'

'So, what have I done to deserve this?' Jacob eyed her suspiciously.

'Well, you're letting me stay until after Christmas, and I'm eating your food…' Tabitha said.

'Tabs, there's no way I had the ingredients for aubergine cannelloni – I've never bought an aubergine in my life.'

'Whatever,' Tabitha said, waving him away from the oven, where the cannelloni were almost ready. 'Help me set the table, I'm starving.'

As Tabitha used kitchen tongs to put the cannelloni on their plates, Jacob observed her closely. She looked tired, but…happy was the word which fitted best, whereas he knew he just looked tired.

'I can't move,' Jacob groaned half an hour later.

'Good, 'cos I want to have a nice long chat,' Tabitha told him.

'You're not going to lecture me, are you?' Jacob asked,

dramatically glancing around for a possible escape route.

'Hardly. Me, lecture you? No, I think you'll find it might be the other way round,' she said, unsmiling.

What? Tabitha never did anything wrong. She was perfect. Straight-A student, entrepreneur, highly successful, achieved everything she set out to do and more besides. Jacob remained silent whilst Tabitha composed herself.

Eventually she just came out with it. 'I'm pregnant.'

Jacob stared at her in disbelief, unable to make the words come. *Pregnant? How? Who? When? I mean I know the how, but she doesn't even have a boyfriend.* 'Pregnant? You're having a baby?' he blurted out.

'Yep. I'm twelve weeks. I just had my scan the other day.' She leant forward and passed him a piece of paper – a sonogram. His nephew or niece.

Taking the picture in his hands, he inspected the little collection of cells outlined on it. Yes, you could just make out that that was the head and that was possibly the curve of its back and those were its legs. My God, Tabitha was having a baby! 'This is so real,' Jacob managed, stroking the scan picture.

Unable to keep her smile in check, Tabitha said, 'I know.'

'So you're happy about it?' Jacob asked her, although what he really wanted to know was who the father was.

'Of course, look at it – it's beautiful and about the size of a passion fruit now.'

Jacob knew there was a joke to be made there, but decided now was not the time. 'So, do you know what it is yet?'

'Yes. It's a baby,' she teased. 'No, you can't tell that until much later, but I don't want to know. Finding out on the day will be enough for me.'

'Good.' Jacob's mind was still racing, trying to work out if Tabitha had told him she was seeing anyone, or even sleeping with anyone, but he drew a blank. 'So,' he came straight out with it, 'does the father know?'

Tabitha hesitated before saying, 'Not yet, but I'll tell him.'

'So, you're not together any more?'

Twisting her hair into a French roll, as she often did when agitated, Tabitha said, 'Well, we were never actually together. He's a client.'

'Oh, Tabs.'

'I know, never mix business and pleasure. Pity I didn't follow my own mantra this time,' she said, pain etched on her face.

'Is he–' Jacob didn't know how to or if he should broach this subject, but finally plumped for '–available?'

'Well done on your subtlety, but I can see through you, remember?' Tabitha said to him. 'That would be too easy and I never do anything the easy way, do I? He's married with two kids.'

'Shit!'

'I know. Never mind. I will tell him, but I'll make it clear I don't want anything from him. I'm not out to wreck his family life and it's not as if I need his money.'

Jacob nodded in agreement. Tabitha had always been self-sufficient. Rising from the sofa, he went over to her and hugged her. 'Tabs, apart from it not being an ideal situation, I'm so happy for you. You'll be a great mum and I get to be an uncle!' He kissed her on the cheek. 'Congratulations.'

'Thanks, you also get to be godfather.'

Jacob had a lump in his throat. 'Really?'

'Well, who better?' Tabitha asked, as she smoothed

down her dress where it had rumpled from Jacob leaning over her.

'Oh, because I'm such a good role model – successful, an achiever...' but Tabitha broke in, 'Stop that self-pitying crap. You're a kind, loving, grounded person who is exactly the role model he or she will need.' She sang a line from a well-known song by The Beatles.

Jacob laughed then and put his arm around her. 'Well, I'll certainly give the baby plenty of love. So have you thought about where you're going to stay once the baby comes?'

'Ah, I'm glad you brought that up. I was hoping we could stay here.'

Chapter Seventeen

14 December

'Thanks,' Meredith told her sister, as she opened the car door for her. Although the hospital had allowed her to be discharged, it was under strict conditions. Since she had no-one at home to care for her, they had only agreed when Amelia, Meredith's sister, had said she would be coming to her house to stay for as long as it took her to recover. She had already prepared the guest room. As Meredith walked slowly up the remaining few steps of Amelia's house to the front door, she drank in its extraordinary beauty: wooden, glass-fronted, a mix of Scandinavian and Italian, but paying homage to the countryside.

Amelia had even tried to get on *Grand Designs* when they were building the house, just for fun, but the programmers told her they had recently shot an episode in Scotland, so it would be some time before there would be another, and Amelia and her husband, Gareth, hadn't wanted to delay the build. But it was the view which was the most impressive, open panoramas over Loch Lomond from three sides of the house; it truly was stunning.

Inside it was no less striking: underfloor heating in the bathrooms, the ultra-modern kitchen with only the Aga hinting at the traditional, the high-ceilinged, wooden-beamed, airy bedrooms with dressing rooms attached, and marble lined the hallway. No expense had been spared and the result was quite something. It was a fantastic home in which to bring up the kids, too, as they had their own zones within the house; a play room, a den of their own, as well as there being a family area where everyone gathered in the evening and at weekends. There Gareth would read the newspaper whilst the children did their homework or watched TV, and Amelia read her book or did the crossword; it was family heaven, but something else entirely for a single person.

Meredith wasn't used to such noise, activity or untidiness. When they entered, Max, three, was lying on his tummy using crayons to draw in his Peppa Pig colouring book; Edward, seven, was slumped on the sofa playing his tablet computer with about six or seven empty sweet papers strewn on the sofa cushion beside him; Alannah's foot was tapping against the coffee table, where she nearly knocked over a glass of juice which was perched close to the edge of the table, as she sang along to whatever tune was playing on her iPod. Having ear buds in meant she had no idea how out of tune she was. At eleven, she was the second eldest; and then there was Jasper, who was reading, and remarkably seemed able to concentrate amid all the chaos. But then, Meredith supposed he must be used to it. She wasn't. She felt quite ill at the prospect of having to chat with all these people, even if they were her nephews and niece.

Fortunately Amelia knew Meredith well, despite the fact they didn't spend a great deal of time together, and she saw how overwhelming and bewildering it all was for her.

'Let's go into the kitchen,' she said, once she had greeted her clan with a kiss on the head each, to cries of, 'Get off,

Mum!' from some and a hug from others.

'Sit yourself down,' Amelia said, 'and I'll make us some tea. Would you like anything to eat?'

Meredith shook her head. She would have preferred coffee, but Amelia had suggested tea. Unlike her usual self, she didn't argue the point; she didn't have the energy. Glancing around her sister's kitchen, it occurred to her how homely everything looked and as if it got used. She thought of her own kitchen, which contained so many items that she had barely taken out of the box. Her coffee machine was the only gadget she really put to good use. Her kitchen work surfaces shone, mainly because of her cleaner and perhaps because she rarely dirtied them.

As she watched Amelia make tea, a sense of calm descended over her. The kitchen was like an oasis set apart from the madness of the rest of the house. She remembered that the guest bedroom was at the back and was grateful for that. Perhaps she could read or work on her laptop in peace there.

'Did you have someone stop by my office to pick up my laptop, like I asked?'

'Nope,' Amelia replied cheerily, 'the doctor said you have to rest and he meant it. You're burnt-out, which is why you got sick in the first place.'

Amelia could be as bossy as Meredith when she set her mind to it. Meredith had no-one to take care of her and although Amelia would hate to be termed a busybody, she would interfere if the situation called for it – like now.

Meredith didn't know whether to be incensed or grateful. In some ways it would be nice to have a break, something she never did, but in others, she had a company to run, and Sophie, for all she was a great assistant, knew nothing about running a company.

'I have a company to run,' she reminded Amelia.

'Yes, yes, I know. Do you think this hasn't happened to anyone before, especially those with their own companies? Well, it has, and doctor's orders are doctor's orders, otherwise you'll risk having a relapse and going back into hospital. So you see, it makes sense just to rest now,' came Amelia's sage response.

Meredith could see the truth in that, but surely it couldn't be good for her health for her to be feeling so anxious about what was happening to the company whilst she was gone?

'It'll be fine.' Amelia broke into her thoughts, reading her mind. 'I've spoken to Sophie and we're working this out together. She can handle most things and if she can't and no-one in the office can, she'll let me know. So far she hasn't needed to contact me. See?'

Should she be insulted or delighted that her staff didn't feel they needed her? Maybe she could take an occasional day off, then, if they felt they could cope? But she knew that it was she who had problems letting go of the reins.

Sipping the tea that Amelia put in front of her, she decided she had to concentrate on getting better. She knew she was a long way from being fit and well, so the most important thing was to recuperate as quickly as possible, so she could get back to work.

'Do you have anything I could read?' she asked Amelia, her expectations low.

'Well, what kind of books do you like? I have chick lit, crime, thrillers, non-fiction. Any of those do you?'

She did like a good thriller, or she had when she'd last read a book a few years ago – the last time she'd taken time for herself.

'A thriller would be great, thanks.'

'Give me a minute. Gareth finished one last night. I think he left it in the living room. Said it was fantastic.'

Meredith watched Amelia's retreating back, then heard her talking to the children. A few barely audible groans emanated from them in response, then she returned with the book. 'There you go.'

'Thanks. I'm quite tired, actually.' She yawned then said, 'I think I'll go up to my room for a while.'

'Come on, then, I'll show you where everything is. No, leave your bag, I'll get it,' said Amelia. 'You've not to overdo it.'

Meredith mumbled her thanks again and climbed the stairs to the guest room. When Amelia told her to go in, she opened the door and was greeted with a profusion of flowers: roses, lilies – maybe not the best choice given their association with funerals, but still sweet of her, and chrysanthemums, placed in a lovely arrangement on the dressing table.

'What lovely flowers,' Meredith said, surprising herself.

'Yes, Alannah made the bouquet for you,' Amelia explained. 'She's very good. She always does ours, too. I'm rubbish, and she insisted on making a special arrangement for you coming to stay.'

Meredith was touched. So, her sullen, monosyllabic niece could be sweet and unselfish? She had barely said two words to Meredith when she arrived. In fact she hadn't said two words, she'd only said hi then returned to her foot tapping.

As Meredith surveyed her surroundings, taking in the pristine quilted hundred per cent cotton comforter, the abundance of pillows and the immaculate guest room she had been given, she thought, *Maybe this won't be so bad after all.*

Chapter Eighteen

16 December

The cry of, 'Sheba! Come here, girl,' woke Meredith. She had now been at Amelia's house for just shy of forty-eight hours and no-one had come to blows and there had been no icy silences nor awkward moments. Mostly she had slept. The children had behaved beautifully, playing out in the garden when the rain was off and playing indoors but more quietly than usual when the weather dictated.

Meredith recognised the voice as Jasper's. Over the past few days she'd worked out that Jasper was the one who mainly walked the dog. Meredith had never owned a dog, although she did like them, and in fact her family had always had dogs when she was growing up. Amelia had continued the tradition with her children, and the golden retriever was clearly an important part of the family.

Meredith joined the family for meals and sometimes to watch a bit of TV together. She had a TV in her room, but she discovered she wanted the company; she wanted to see what the children were doing. Being surrounded by children was a novelty for her and she found them quite endearing in their own full-on, one hundred miles an hour way. She wrapped her bathrobe around herself and made her way downstairs.

The scene which greeted her was one of chaos: four children, three of them in school uniform, digging into bowls of cereal, munching pieces of buttered toast and coaxing pieces of egg out of their egg cups. Sheba lay at the foot of one of the chairs, whilst Max, the youngest, tried to chew round his toast, without actually eating it. The previously immaculate kitchen was anything but. Worktops were covered in lunchboxes, with various pieces of fruit, packets of raisins and sandwiches with the crusts cut off lined up in rows, as if on parade. A pile of dirty clothes was heaped in front of the washing machine – towels from the children's showers that morning and their pyjamas, except Max's. He was still wearing his. Toast crumbs, marmalade-covered knives and Pokemon figures graced the breakfast table.

Far from turning around and walking away in disgust as she would normally have done, Meredith pulled up a chair and sat down with them. The children immediately started firing questions at her. Her favourite had to be Edward's: 'So how come it's new monia and not old monia?' At this point his mother interjected and gave him a bit of a spelling lesson before explaining the meaning of the word. Meredith smiled. Maybe Amelia had the right idea. She was surrounded by people who loved her, had a nice lifestyle and a husband who adored her. *Am I missing out?*

The weekend had been a long one, and miserable weather too, which Stanley often felt went a long way to setting your mood. He had been glad when Monday had come around again. The outing to the pub the other night with a few of his friends from the club had done him the world of good; hopefully they could do it again soon. Stanley had noticed that not everyone came to the club every day, or even on the three days that he did. Many had to pay for it, particularly if they had private pensions. Stanley felt that was unfair, even though he didn't have to pay. Forty pounds a day seemed pretty steep to him. Who would have that kind of money? But apparently there were a few; not that you'd know to look at them. They didn't seem any different from him. Or maybe they were widowers, too. That went a long way to explaining why a man wasn't as well-turned-out as he could be, particularly if his wife had done everything for him whilst she was alive.

Lunch had been quite tasty again: broccoli soup, chicken pie with potatoes and peas, and rhubarb crumble to finish. He certainly couldn't make that himself, so he was delighted to have a good square meal at least once a day. Thinking back to Edie's cooking always made him smile – she had been a wonderful cook, plain food, but she enjoyed making it and it shone through in the end result. Lucky wasn't the word for how he considered himself – all those wonderful years together. He'd always assumed he would shuffle off this mortal coil first. Life had a way of teaching you, he thought, that not everything could be planned as you expected.

Stanley had worked out that on Mondays people had a little bit less verve. They preferred a more leisurely day at the club, reading or doing the crossword. The domino tournaments and debates were more likely to happen midweek onwards. So he had followed suit that morning and read his book quietly, occasionally talking to one of the other members.

Although traditionally after lunch they were all a bit sleepy, today was an exception. Cathy had told them earlier that she had some news to share with them, so the members were all trying to work out what it could be. Some guessed they were moving the club, others that they were changing the hours, or the transport, but no-one guessed the real reason.

'Right, everyone.' Cathy's voice boomed around the room. 'I'm going to draw the raffle for the fundraiser we did for you, and I need a few volunteers to pick out the tickets.'

A few hands shot up and as Cathy walked around, hands delved into the depths of the bucket to pull out winning tickets. The top prize was a Christmas hamper, donated by the local butcher. It went to a Mrs P Dean from Aberfoyle. None of the members won anything and there was a great deal of grumbling about that until Cathy said, 'I also have an announcement to make. We managed to raise the grand total of six hundred and seventy-five pounds, and Crilly's Hotel down the road had a last-minute cancellation, so you'll be having a Christmas party. Get your Sunday best looked out!'

At this, applause broke out and then the members gave three cheers for Cathy, who had masterminded the fundraiser.

Blushing, she said, 'You deserve it. Just behave yourselves. I don't want you all getting blitzed and me having to carry you home.'

Laughter rang out and the mood within the room brightened, eclipsing the gloomy weather outside.

As Cathy told them all the date and time of the party, Stanley had a little inner monologue with Edie. She approved of the club and was glad to see him getting out and about, enjoying himself. It would be something to look forward to.

Across town, Rebecca smoothed down her new skirt and

removed a piece of imaginary lint from her matching jacket. It had taken her and Hannah only three hours on Saturday to find the perfect outfit for the interview. Navy, as opposed to dreary black, bias cut.

She had arrived for her interview fifteen minutes early, only to find another two candidates waiting. 'Mr Melbourne's running a little late,' the receptionist advised her when she stated who she was. 'Please take a seat.'

Rebecca ran over and over in her head what she wanted to convey to Dominic Melbourne so he knew she was the right person for the role. What would it take to persuade him she ought to be his new assistant manager?

The interviews didn't last long, as each candidate before her was in and out in less than twenty minutes. Finally Rebecca's name was called, and she rapped on the door to Mr Melbourne's office and was invited to come in.

As soon as she shook Dominic's hand, she immediately liked him. She knew she would do a great job for him, and he quickly put her at ease. She thought she had given intelligent answers to all of his questions and when he asked her if she had any of her own, she came up with pertinent, well-researched ones which demonstrated her knowledge of the art world.

Dominic's comments were encouraging, so she was a little subdued when he said only that he would be in touch.

What did I expect, that he would offer me the job on the spot? Rebecca scolded herself as she opened her car door and slumped onto the driver's seat. She felt as if someone had just pricked a hole in her balloon. But this was the first opportunity of any merit which had presented itself in such a long time – this job was hers; it had to be. So why didn't it feel as if it was going to happen? Both the telephone interview and the face-to-face one had gone really well, but there was a lack of commitment on Dominic's side which worried her, unless he just had a good poker face. Chastising herself for her negativity and trying to convince herself that Dominic was just being a professional and interviewing the rest of the candidates first before making any decisions, she headed home.

As Rebecca made dinner that night, it occurred to her that her interview had lasted an hour and a half, more than an hour longer than the two previous candidates'. Surely that boded well.

Chapter Nineteen

17 December

A baby. He was going to be an uncle. And Tabitha wanted them both to stay with him! Had he imagined that part? But no, Tabitha had been very clear. She thought they would rub along well together and quite frankly she needed him. How was she supposed to take care of a baby on her own? She could hire a nanny, but she had said she preferred to keep it in the family. Working part-time from home and having Jacob for support in the evenings and weekends would allow her to do that. Given that their parents hadn't been around for them, she didn't want to repeat that mistake with her child, she'd told him.

Initially Jacob had been gobsmacked, but now he'd had time to get used to the idea, he was warming to it. He loved children and hoped to have some of his own someday – obviously after finding a partner with whom to have them. He didn't need to worry about girls right now, he wasn't on their radar, but if Tabitha and the baby did move in, he'd have even less chance of getting a girlfriend. He could hardly take a girl back to his, when they might be disturbed in the throes of passion by *Wah wah!* Throes of passion, he could barely remember what they were. He'd be as well in a monastery for all the action he saw, and his latest rejection by Rebecca, no matter what the reason, hadn't helped his self-esteem.

After having slept on it, and reflected upon it at length, Jacob had decided that it would be a brilliant idea to have his sister and niece or nephew live with him. He'd always wanted that sense of family which his parents had been unable to give him and Tabitha. He wanted the next generation to be surrounded by love and their relatives.

'So how does that thing work?' Meredith asked Edward. So, seven-year-old Edward showed her how to play *Super Mario* on his games console.

Within forty minutes Meredith was entering new worlds, capturing keys and arguing with Edward good-naturedly about whose turn it was. An hour later, laying down the device, she said, 'That was fun. Amelia, OK if I use the phone?'

Amelia nodded and when asked if she had a Yellow Pages replied that it lived in the rack of the phone table. Meredith smiled; Amelia must be one of the few people who still possessed a phone table. Those had gone out of fashion aeons ago with the advent of cordless phones. Long gone was the banishment to the hall to sit in the freezing cold to make or take a call.

Meredith sat on the chair beside the phone table, looked up Sugar and Spice in the Yellow Pages and rang the number. After four rings, a voice she recognised answered. 'Sugar and Spice, Natalie speaking.'

'Hello, Natalie, this is Meredith Storm.'

'Oh hello, Meredith. How are you feeling?'

'Much better, thank you, although I've been told to take it easy for a while.'

'Quite right, too. You've got to treat these illnesses with

respect.'

'Yes. Anyway, I was just phoning to thank you for your quick thinking last week. I really appreciate it.'

'You're most welcome. We hope to see you in here when you're better.'

'Well, I might come myself occasionally and allow Sophie to get on with some work,' Meredith thought out loud. 'Oh, and can you tell the young man who works with you…'

'Jacob,' Natalie broke in.

'Yes, Jacob. Can you thank him from me, too, for calling the ambulance?'

'I will do.'

'Well, I'll let you go. I know you must be busy. It really is a great little bakery and those Christmas specials you've been making are delicious.'

'Thank you. I'm so glad you enjoyed them.'

'Well, take care,' Meredith finished awkwardly.

'You too, goodbye, Meredith.'

Natalie replaced the receiver.

Well, well, well, she thought.

Meredith had another task she needed to address and she was running out of time. She usually spent weeks or months selecting gifts for her family. It was the one family-centric activity to which she gave her full attention. She dialled her office number, and the receptionist, after asking how she was, put her straight through to Sophie.

After enlisting Sophie's help, Meredith began to make notes in her indecipherable, loopy scrawl.

Jasper – an e-reader. He'd mentioned that he'd broken the screen on his and that was why he was reading a paperback. Although personally Meredith preferred to read paper books, she could see the attraction, particularly for the younger generation, and if it got them reading, that could only be a good thing.

Edward – Nintendo games.

Alannah – Alannah had expressed an interest in listening to music like they did 'in the olden days', so Meredith chose a turntable and indicated she wanted a selection of albums of hit artists through the decades.

Max – since she had arrived at Amelia's, she had noticed that Max was absolutely nuts about Peppa Pig, so much so that his parents acted out the parts of Mummy and Daddy Pig, much to Meredith's amusement and Alannah and Jasper's horror. Edward was still young enough to find it funny. So for Max, something Peppa Pig-related. Sophie would know better than her what to get – difficult to choose without being able to physically see the toys on offer.

Amelia – Amelia had everything she could ever want, but Meredith thought perhaps a weekend at Gleneagles for her and Gareth, as well as a dress for her sister, similar to one worn by a model on a TV show they'd watched together the other night and which Amelia had said was gorgeous.

Gareth – a 'swimming with sharks' experience. He'd always said he'd fancied it. Now he'd have to man up and prove if he'd been kidding them on all along. Personally Meredith thought he was serious about it. Now was his chance.

Even Sheba the golden retriever would get a present, a spa day for dogs. Jasper would probably thank her for that most, since he seemed to take care of her almost exclusively.

Meredith knew that Amelia had twenty-one people coming for Christmas dinner, including their parents, her in-laws, and cousins on Gareth's side, so she added a few little presents to the list: Belgian chocolates, a couple of bottles of champagne, two silk ties, as well as a Barbie doll and a wooden train set. Well before Sophie arrived to take charge of the list, Meredith was able to sit back and admire it as a job well done.

'Which garden centre did you buy the tree at?' Jacob asked Natalie just before closing that day.

'Oh, it was the one on Loch Road,' said Natalie. 'Not got your tree up yet?'

'No,' Jacob started to explain, then changed what he was going to say to, 'You know, with Tabitha arriving and her news, I haven't had time yet.'

'Well, you don't want to wait much longer, or you won't get the best out of it.'

'I know, I'm going to call in on the way home, see if they can deliver it tonight or tomorrow night.'

Once Jacob and she had parted ways, heading for opposite ends of town, Natalie smiled. She knew why Jacob hadn't seen fit to put his tree up yet, but was glad to see he now felt the time had arrived.

Chapter Twenty

18 December

The phone rang just as Stanley was coming in the front door. He didn't even have time to pick up the mail lying behind it. Even with his stick to aid him, he couldn't move particularly quickly at the best of times, with his arthritis, but he always tried to reach a ringing phone. You never knew if it could be important. The climb up the four flights of stairs had worn him out, too. He'd been on the housing list to get a house on the level for the past eight years, but still nothing. He reached the phone and said a breathless, 'Hello?'

'Grandpa, it's me.'

'Thomas, my boy, how are you?' Stanley's breathlessness and tiredness were long forgotten, as he revelled in the rare phone call from his only grandson.

'I'm good, Grandpa, how are you?'

'Oh, you know, not bad, son. So what have you been up to?'

'I have something to tell you. I'm getting married.'

'Aw, congratulations, son, that's great news. When's the big day?'

'Christmas Eve,' Thomas informed him.

'That's next week!'

'I know. It's been a bit hectic getting everything organised.'

Stanley sat down on his chair with the cordless phone and said, 'I would have loved to be there, son, but you know how things are.'

'I do, Grandpa, and I really wanted you there,' his grandson admitted.

Stanley was touched.

'That's why we decided to get married in Scotland.'

'What?' Stanley almost fell off his chair. 'You're coming here?'

'Yep. Catherine and I decided we wanted to get married on Loch Lomond, even though it will be freezing,' he said.

'Oh son, I can't believe it. That's fantastic news! When are you coming?'

'Our flight's the day after tomorrow. We're going to bring in the New Year in Scotland, too.'

'You don't know how happy you've just made me,' Stanley said, openly weeping now.

'Grandpa, don't cry. I think Mum and Dad would have wanted this, too. We hoped we could spend Christmas Day with you, before we spend a bit of time on our Scottish honeymoon.'

'That would be wonderful.' Stanley could barely get the words out, tears flowing openly down his face.

Once the details had been discussed, Stanley hung up and cast his eyes skywards. 'Thank you, Edie.'

He knew his angel had looked after him – now he wouldn't be alone this Christmas.

'I managed to get everything on the list.' Sophie handed a bunch of receipts and invoices to Meredith, as well as a bundle of gifts. As per Meredith's instructions, she'd also bought masses of fancy silver and gold wrapping paper, bows, ribbons, and more gift-wrapping paraphernalia than she thought one person could ever need. Personalised cards had also been created and only needed Meredith to include her special message inside each one.

'I didn't doubt it.' Meredith smiled at her and Sophie almost passed out from the shock.

Meredith knew how to smile? She must really be ill.

'Thanks for this.' Meredith gestured to the bundles beside her.

It took all of Sophie's resolve for her legs not to give way beneath her.

'No problem,' she said, returning Meredith's smile. It felt a bit weird, smiling at Cruella, but for some reason also kind of right. She was a diminished Cruella right now; almost human.

Chapter Twenty-one

19 December

'This arrived for you.' Amelia placed a box on Meredith's bedside table.

'What is it?' Meredith asked, furrowing her brow. She wasn't expecting anything. Sophie had bought everything she'd requested and nothing was being delivered directly here, just in case it was intercepted by nosy children.

'No idea. Courier just dropped it off.'

Meredith undid the voluminous transparent wrapping paper which housed a pale pink box. Peering closely at it, she saw the box was emblazoned with the logo, Sugar and Spice. She opened it to find a selection of miniature cakes. An envelope lay on top. Meredith opened the envelope, took out the note it contained, read it and smiled.

Since you can't come to us, we didn't want you to miss out on our Christmas cakes. Here are miniature versions of those you've missed. Get well soon, Natalie and Jacob.

Meredith reread the note and then noticed it was wet. Confused, she suddenly realised tears were running down her face. *People can be very good*, she thought. She dried her eyes, picked up the box and headed downstairs to share the cakes with her family.

Stanley admired himself in the mirror. He had been all for wearing his kilt, but had spoken to George the night before, who had advised him that might make him a tad overdressed, particularly as their party was during the day. Stanley had conceded that was true and had chosen instead a navy blazer and teamed that with a pair of smart navy trousers. His tie was gold and navy, and he combed his hair until he deemed himself presentable. For some reason it felt of paramount importance that he make an effort. Edie would be watching.

Another manic day at Sugar and Spice. Tabitha had been in to sample some of the Christmas cakes, moaning Jacob never brought her any home, but in reality to get her out of the house and mixing with people. She had registered with the medical practice and the midwife in the town, as a first crucial step to moving in permanently with her brother. Neither Tabitha nor Jacob felt the need to inform their parents. It wasn't as if they were in regular contact and the last e-mail had indicated they would spend Christmas in Dubai, courtesy of Sheik Rashid bin Khalifa. Tabitha hadn't even seen fit to tell her parents they were to become grandparents. She couldn't bear the thought of the lecture, and she didn't exactly expect them to be ecstatic, so she felt it was fair enough to let them wait.

As Meredith observed Amelia with her youngest son, the obvious bond between them melted her usually icy heart. *She really does have it all figured out, doesn't she?*
As the three of them munched on some of the miniature cakes, the adults exclaiming how divine they were and Max voicing, 'Yum!' occasionally, Meredith began to realise she didn't want to go back to the way things had

been before. It was time to make some changes, drastic ones.

At Crilly's Hotel, the pensioners' Christmas party was in full swing. The caterers had excelled themselves and Cathy and her team had arrived earlier that day to decorate the function suite with Christmas banners, balloons, baubles and even a *piñata* – old people were just like children – they enjoyed party games, although musical chairs was obviously out, as some would have issues getting out of the chairs at all, and the game would last an exceedingly long time. They did, however, manage Pass the Parcel. The strains of forties' and fifties' music could be heard coming from the hotel's sound system. Cathy and Betty had made it their business to get it right, by asking the pensioners over the course of the past ten days who their favourite musicians were.

Lunch was grander than their usual affair at the club, even though the quality there was also pretty good – Cathy and her gang made sure of that. But the caterers really had done a first-class job. Quails eggs on toast; chicken liver paté with oatcakes, or smoked salmon made up the starters. Turkey with all the trimmings, roast lamb with winter vegetables and roast potatoes, or ham with the same accompaniments constituted the main event. The dessert menu consisted of homemade apple pie, for those with a less adventurous palate; white chocolate and raspberry cheesecake, or sticky toffee and date pudding with lashings of creamy custard.

After lunch Stanley and his friends sang along and those who were able to, danced, to their heroes and heroines. Ella Fitzgerald, Duke Ellington, Bing Crosby's 'White Christmas', Billie Holiday, Frank Sinatra, Peggy Lee and

Perry Como were some of those who brought back happy memories. For Stanley's part, the song which reminded him most of Edie was Frank Sinatra's 'I've Got You Under My Skin', and as he watched men and women dance to it, he smiled and remembered how she had looked then. Beautiful – with her poodle cut she'd reminded him of Audrey Hepburn in *Roman Holiday*. He preferred to think of her now as she had been as a young woman and not the older one who had been ravaged by the disease that had ultimately taken her. They had shared so many good times and Stanley knew he was a lucky man. He hoped with all his heart that his grandson and his bride-to-be could have even half the happiness he had experienced with his beloved wife.

At Amelia's, Meredith was scribbling away in a small notebook she carried in her bag. A picture was forming in her mind of how the future could be, if she let go of the reins even a little. Some time for herself would be a good start. Maybe eventually she'd entertain the idea of someone special in her life again. Witnessing the harmony amid the bedlam of her sister's home, Meredith had come to realise that she wasn't quite so against disorder as she had first thought. It had its place. Although she couldn't quite reconcile herself to the idea of having children, and quite frankly she was probably too old now, she could still have a family life; she could be a more hands-on aunt, and what better time to start than Christmas? Amelia had already made it clear Meredith wouldn't be going back to her own flat until the New Year, and if she tried, Amelia would put in a call to her doctor, who would recommend she go back into hospital.

Suddenly Meredith was looking forward to Christmas,

imagining what it would be like watching the children open their presents, their little excited faces when they asked if Santa had been. Of course, the older two knew that Santa didn't exist, but Edward and Max were still little enough to believe.

Meredith sketched out some ideas for the company – nothing to stress her out. If anything, she was sure the doctor would approve. Even putting pen to paper in this way seemed to make any remaining stress flow out of her; the exercise in itself was cathartic.

You were never too old to receive a present from Santa, it appeared. Not all of the money raised for the party had been spent, so Cathy had decided they should buy each of the members a small gift, nothing fancy, just a wee minding. Stanley was delighted with his book about Scottish birds. It had been a long time since he'd done any serious bird-watching, but perhaps next year. With free bus travel throughout Scotland, he could take a day trip somewhere and see if he could spot some of the rarer birds in his book. Receiving his present reminded Stanley he still had to wrap the gifts he had bought for his grandson and Catherine.

They were arriving later that night, but they would meet up with him only the next day, Thomas had explained on the phone, as their flight landed at eleven. That would give Stanley plenty of time to wrap their presents and have some nice things in for lunch when they called round. He hadn't been to Sugar and Spice for a while. He'd pick up some nice bread and some cakes there in the morning, but right now, it was time for his brain to rejoin the party.

Cathy was walking around with a box and everyone was taking a piece of paper from it. Intrigued, Stanley reached his hand in when the box came to him. He opened his piece of paper and saw the phrase 'doon the water'.

'What I'd like you all to do is tell us a story from your life, or an event that has happened to you, related to the word or phrase on your piece of paper. I'll give you a few minutes to have a think about it.' Cathy beamed at them all.

Some of the pensioners looked puzzled until Cathy said, 'C'mon you lot, you've all been around for a long time. There must be at least one story that fits!'

At this the old folk began to laugh. Stanley studied the piece of paper again and cast his mind back to 1947. The *Waverley* paddle steamer; a splendid vessel – the last of its kind, as it turned out. They'd caught it from Craigendoran in Helensburgh across to Arrochar on Loch Long. Such a glorious day – not a cloud in the sky. The sun made the ripples in the water flash like jewels, but not quite as much as the diamond before him – his Edie. He had joked with her over her choice of clothing, a dress to go on the *Waverley* – she'd be soaked. She didn't care. She had got drenched but had laughed it off. So it was that Stanley, to an incredibly damp Edie, had got down on one knee and produced a small navy velvet box. Edie's hand had flown to her throat in shock, then she had gazed into Stanley's eyes, as she waited for him to ask her the question.

'Will you marry me, Edie?'

'Yes, yes and three times, yes!' They had clung to each other and had kissed passionately as onlookers cheered. They'd left the *Waverley* with their arms around each other's waists.

Over the years they'd been on the *Waverley* many times and had travelled on all its routes. But none of the occasions had ever been as special as that day. The last time they had sailed on her had been the year before, a round trip from

Glasgow to Tighnabruaich. Edie had known that would be her last trip, but instead of being sorrowful about it, she embraced it, almost becoming for a second that girl from 1947.

As Stanley told his story, there wasn't a dry eye in the room.

Chapter Twenty-two

20 December

'Grandpa!' Thomas hugged his grandfather, who clung on a little tighter than was necessary.

Stanley took Thomas's face in his hands and kissed him on both cheeks. 'You look just like your father.'

'I know, everyone's always telling me so.'

'He was a fine-looking man.'

'Yeah, he was.'

'Catherine, my girl. You look wonderful, even better than in the photographs.'

'Thanks, lovely to meet you, Mr Winters.'

'Oh, please call me Stanley. We don't stand on ceremony around here. Talking of which, tell me about this wedding of yours whilst I make us a wee bite to eat. Sandwiches OK?'

'You don't need to bother, Grandpa. We don't want to put you to any trouble. We can grab something later.'

'Nonsense, it's not every day your only grandson comes to visit you, and better still arranges to get married on your doorstep. Roast beef, cheese or ham?'

Thomas and Catherine both plumped for roast beef and Stanley whistled as he prepared the sandwiches and put the kettle on to boil. The cakes from Sugar and Spice he presented on a little silver cake rack Edie had always loved.

As they ate lunch in Stanley's tiny dining room, the happy couple told him all about the plans for their wedding on Loch Lomond and informed him that they would be staying at Aberlomond House Hotel. Stanley thought he might get the use of his kilt this year after all.

Rebecca had been glad she was only working a half day, as it meant she could have a lie-in. The postman woke her around ten and she lay under the covers basking in the fact she didn't need to get up just yet. Eventually, her needing the loo overcame her desire to stay in bed and she ventured out, picking up her letters from the mat in the hall onto which they had fallen. Electricity bill, mobile phone bill, credit card bill…wait a minute, The Melbourne Gallery. Her heart racing, Rebecca held the envelope to her, almost scrunching it up in the process. This was it – yes or no. A major change in her life, or the usual humdrum job for the foreseeable future. Rebecca opened the envelope. Nestling inside on The Melbourne Gallery headed paper, complete with navy embossed logo, was a single sheet of A4, followed by a thick document.

Dear Miss Cowan

*Further to your recent interview and after careful consideration of an extensive candidate list…*Rebecca's heart sank. She hadn't got it. There had been too many other well-qualified candidates. Steeling herself, she read on, *'we are delighted to offer you the position as Assistant Manager of The Melbourne Gallery. Please call Mr Melbourne directly to arrange a start date. Your contract is enclosed. Please read your terms and conditions carefully, sign and date both copies and return one copy to us in the envelope provided.*

Yours faithfully
Janine Burns (PA to Dominic Melbourne)

She'd got it! She'd got it! She couldn't believe it. Dancing around the living room, waving the letter in the air, Rebecca almost hurdled the coffee table. She jumped up and down on the sofa, then bounced off and immediately called Hannah.

A gurgling noise came over the phone. 'Hannah? Are you gargling with mouthwash or something?'

'No, I'm in Glasgow, just heading into the underground. How you doing?'

'Fan-bloody-tastic! I got the job! I got the bloody job!'

'Becks, that's fantastic! Well done. I knew you could do it.'

'I can't believe it.' Rebecca still had difficulty taking it in.

'Well, you deserve it. Congratulations. Listen, I can't hear you that well. I'll call you later, so we can go celebrate.'

'No worries.' Rebecca hung up and stared again at the letter. Here was real cause for celebration. She had two calls to make. One to Dominic and the second to Ethan. She wanted to keep the flat now. With the extra salary, she could afford it.

You couldn't move in Sugar and Spice for exhausted shoppers laden down with overflowing shopping bags. Jacob and Natalie were rushed off their feet, but they were in fine festive spirit, and so it seemed were the tired shoppers. Only five more days until Christmas. Jacob was going to have to buy Tabitha's present on Sunday, as it was his only day off. He decided he ought to buy a gift for Natalie, too, but what? And it wasn't as if he was flush with cash, and what if she felt awkward if she hadn't bought him something? But they were such a team, the two of them, so he wanted to buy her a little something.

Natalie was overjoyed; everything was coming together. Rebecca had popped in earlier and sworn her to secrecy as she picked up a coffee and a piece of cake to go. She'd got the job and said Sugar and Spice had been instrumental in her applying in the first place. Rebecca couldn't thank Natalie enough. Her face radiating with happiness, it was clear that this step up was exactly what she had needed.

Stanley, too, had been in earlier to buy some Irish soda bread and some slices of the day's Christmas cake – *bolo polana* – a cake made from potatoes and cashew nuts, native to Mozambique, and which tasted much better than it sounded, Natalie assured him.

When prompted by Natalie, he'd talked at length about how great the old folks' Christmas party had been. Everyone had deemed it the best Christmas party they'd ever had. They'd all been a little bit tiddled later on, but no-one had been arrested, he'd joked. Stanley had gone on to tell them that his grandson had come over from Canada for Christmas and that wasn't all, he was getting married here on Christmas Eve. It warmed Natalie's heart to see how the old man's face glowed and how the good news had shaved ten years off him. He'd promised to tell the soon-to-be newly-weds about Sugar and Spice and hoped they would come by and try out some more of the speciality cakes.

The Christmas tree was still going strong and the items which adorned it continued to draw comments of approval and questions as to their origin from the bakery's patrons. Two gifts had materialised underneath it. Jacob noticed them but said nothing. On Sunday he'd buy his own.

'Ethan, I can't believe you,' Rebecca almost screamed down the phone. 'It's only been a few days. You know how much I love that flat. I had to convince you it was the right one for us. You weren't even that bothered. Can't you just speak to the lawyer and put it on hold until I can speak to mine?' Rebecca cajoled.

'It's too late, and anyway, I can't just chop and change to suit you. I'm glad you got your promotion. Really, I'm pleased for you, but just let the flat go.'

Rebecca, deflated, hung up. *Thanks, Ethan, you know just how to burst my bubble, as always.*

A day that should have been full only of celebration had now been tinged by disappointment. She knew Ethan; once his mind was made up, there was no changing it.

Chapter Twenty-three

21 December

'So, I thought perhaps we could have a little party here on Monday.' Natalie ran her idea past Jacob. 'What do you think?'

Tabitha, who had become almost a permanent fixture and who subsisted solely on pieces of cake and multiple decaf lattes, interrupted her before Jacob had a chance to answer.

'Did I hear you say party? That's a great idea. I can't go to any proper parties this year. No point. I can't drink. But a party here would be perfect.'

She turned to Jacob to see if he would agree.

Jacob supposed it couldn't do any harm. Tabitha was as excited as a little girl. He began to see what the following year would be like when they would have a baby around at Christmas, although he supposed the baby would be too young to take it all in – the year after, perhaps.

'So what did you have in mind?' asked Jacob, wondering how much more Christmassy they could make the bakery, which was already festooned with holly, mistletoe and Christmas decorations in every possible space, not to forget the sumptuous Christmas tree.

'Well, I thought we could make some special Christmas

treats in miniature – similar to those we made for Meredith – a selection of those we made throughout the month. Those and some sandwiches, sausage rolls, vol au vents, and some hot and cold drinks ought to cover it.'

'But won't that cost a lot of money for all the ingredients?' Jacob frowned.

'Tsk! No. I'll take care of that. I think we give the customers a free afternoon where they can come and try the bakery's wares. That way we might get even more new customers after Christmas.'

At this Jacob looked doubtful, but shrugged. 'You're the boss.'

'Right, that's settled then.' Natalie winked at Tabitha. 'Tabitha, perhaps you can help me come up with some ideas for drinks?'

'Love to.' Tabitha took the piece of paper and the pen Natalie proffered her.

A party. Yes, a party was exactly what was needed, Natalie thought.

Sugar and Spice invites you all to its FREE Christmas party – 1pm–5pm

Monday 23 December. Christmas cakes from around the world, prizes, music and plenty of festive cheer. We'd love to see you there.

Sophie read the sign on the door as she pushed it open to go in and have her daily caffeine fix; oh, OK then, she admitted it, her daily sugar fix, too.

What a great idea. I wonder…

When things had quieted down later that afternoon, Natalie called Mrs Williams to see how her progress was going and also to tell her about the party. She didn't want her

hearing about it from another source. She needn't have
worried. Mrs Williams thought it was a wonderful idea and
congratulated Natalie on her quick thinking.

'Why didn't I think of that myself?' she said.

Natalie then broached the other matter she'd called
about. Mrs Williams trusted Natalie's judgement, as she
had heard such good things from her regulars who had
called to check on her well-being or popped in, bringing her
homemade meals, since she was still largely indisposed.

She had no hesitation in agreeing to Natalie's proposal.

'Sophie, come in.' Amelia ushered her in the front door.
'What are you doing here at the weekend?'

'Meredith asked me to come by as she has something
she wants to discuss with me.'

'She didn't mention anything about you stopping by.
Let me take your coat. It's boiling in this house.' She held
out her hand, as Sophie removed her scarf, coat and gloves.

'It's certainly not boiling out there,' Sophie remarked
with a grin. 'But yes, what a difference as soon as you
come in here.'

Sophie was still in awe of Amelia's house. It was like
something out of an interior design magazine. Everything
was so beautiful. She was admiring the cornicing on the
ceiling in the atrium, when a gorgeous golden retriever
almost bowled her over.

'Oh, what a beautiful dog. Come here, boy.' Sophie
scratched Sheba under the chin.

'Girl,' said Jasper, coming up behind Sheba.

'Ah, sorry, girl. She is, though; gorgeous, I mean. Her
coat is so healthy-looking.'

'You a dog person?' Jasper asked, curling Sheba's leash
around his fingers.

'Well, my grandparents always had dogs, although I've never had one myself. I'd love to, but it's just not feasible with the hours I work,' Sophie explained, stroking Sheba's silky coat.

'Ah, there you are,' Meredith said warmly. 'I thought I heard your voice. Amelia, is there somewhere private, apart from my room, where Sophie and I can talk?'

'Sure, use the downstairs study,' Amelia suggested.

'Thanks. So, how are things?' Meredith asked Sophie as they headed towards the study. Sophie noticed Meredith was scrutinising her and she tried not to gulp. She'd always tried to avoid direct eye contact with her in the past when it was clear something was on Meredith's mind. She rarely came off better for it. Sophie began to rhyme off a list of things Meredith might want to know about the goings-on in the company, but Meredith stopped her by raising her hand. 'No, Sophie, how are you?' She smiled. 'How are you coping? You've had a lot to deal with unexpectedly.'

Bewildered, Sophie mumbled that she was fine, just a bit busy. 'So,' Sophie asked, trying to steer the conversation away from herself, 'did you get your presents wrapped?'

'Yes, I did, thanks.'

Still that warm smile. It was quite unnerving when you weren't used to it.

'Did you forget anything?' Sophie asked, wondering if that was why she was here.

'No, I don't think so. Why don't you sit down. I have something I need to talk to you about.'

Truly worried now, Sophie perched on the end of the chair opposite the walnut desk, behind which Meredith now sat, swinging on the leather swivel chair.

'The thing is, Sophie, I've had a chance to think about things, *really* think about things whilst I've been ill…'

Oh God, she's going to sack me.

'And I'm going to be cutting back the hours I'm working, taking the occasional holiday...'

What? Had she heard right? Sophie's eyes were wide with disbelief. Maybe Meredith had suffered more of a bump on the head when she'd fallen than first thought.

'And although I'll be delegating some of my workload to some of the department heads, I was thinking about creating a new position – someone to act as liaison between the department heads and myself.'

Right, Sophie was thinking. *And?*

'I'd like that person to be you. It would include some of the extra stuff you do for me currently, but you would no longer be a PA. In fact one of your first tasks would be to find me another PA. There would be more responsibility and recognition and a considerable increase in pay.'

At the 'considerable increase in pay', Sophie's ears pricked up. Had she heard right? Was Meredith offering her a promotion?

'I hope you'll see this as the step up you deserve, and that you'll accept.' Meredith fixed her once again with that disconcerting stare.

'I-I-I don't know what to say,' Sophie stammered, because honestly she was lost for words. It hadn't occurred to her that Meredith might ever promote her. She had barely tolerated her until last week, hadn't shown her much, if any, respect until then. Maybe she'd had a near-death experience with this bout of pneumonia, that must be it. No doubt Sophie would find herself back as PA in a few weeks' time, but for the moment she'd just humour her.

'That sounds great,' she finally got out.

'Excellent. Here's a list of the items I need you to address ASAP with regard to informing other departments about your new appointment, and I'll leave it to you to choose the correct channels for organising your replacement. Here are the terms of your contract. If you could have someone type that up for me in the company's usual contract-speak and pass it to Legal for authorisation, we'll be good to go.'

Sophie was flabbergasted. It was actually happening. Meredith was finally trusting her with something of her own.

'I-I-I don't know what to say,' she stuttered again.

Meredith said, 'Then say yes.'

'Yes.'

'Good, now that's sorted, there's just one more thing.' Meredith withdrew an envelope from her bag.

'Oh?'

'Your Christmas bonus.'

'But we don't give Christmas bonuses.'

'We do this year, but I'd be grateful if you'd keep the contents of the envelope confidential.'

'Of course. Thank you.'

'No, thank *you*.'

Sophie stood there as if Medusa had turned her to stone.

'Well, aren't you going to open it?'

'What? Oh yes, sorry.' Sophie opened the envelope and withdrew a cheque for five thousand pounds.

That really did render her speechless. She'd reckoned maybe a hundred or even two hundred quid, but five grand? Bloody hell. By the time Meredith uttered the next sentence Sophie had pretty much spent it.

Meredith had seen behind the rosy glow of Sophie's cheeks, due to the cold outside, how pinched her assistant's face really was, the dark circles under her eyes and she knew that Sophie must be running herself ragged in her absence, trying to keep everything ticking over. She was glad she had finally rewarded her and chided herself for not having done so beforehand.

'Jacob, I wanted to talk to you about something,' said Natalie, as she took off her rubber gloves and massaged moisturising cream into her hands, once all the customers had gone.

'OK.'

'I need to head home unexpectedly; family issues.'

'Oh, right.' Jacob was wondering how he would manage on his own until she got back.

As if reading his mind, Natalie said, 'I won't be coming back. I was only ever meant to be here on a short placement. Mrs Williams was meant to be returning to work full-time, but I spoke to her yesterday and she's still not well enough.'

'That's not so good.'

'No, it's not. The thing is, even when she is better, she doesn't want to work full-time, so she's decided to appoint a manager.'

'Oh.' Jacob hoped he would get on as well with the new boss as he did with Natalie. 'So when's the new boss starting, then?'

'He already has.' Natalie smiled expectantly at him.

After a moment's pause, Jacob said, 'Me? But I've only been here two minutes.'

'Well, more like three weeks, but who's counting?' said Natalie. 'The important thing is you know what to do, the customers like you and you're enthusiastic.'

'But I can't bake!'

'Not a problem. Nuala's broken leg is a lot better. She'll be back in on the twenty-seventh to help you and to bake the cakes, but you'll be responsible for everything else, including her.'

With the realisation that this wasn't a wind-up, Jacob grinned.

'Mrs Williams won't regret giving me the chance, I promise you, and thanks. If it wasn't for you, I wouldn't be working here at all.' Jacob gave Natalie's arm a friendly squeeze.

'Nonsense. You did it all by yourself. It was you who plucked up the courage to ask for the job in the first place. All I did was act as intermediary. Anyway, there are things we have to discuss before I work my last day on Christmas Eve, so we had better make a start on your training tomorrow.'

'Sounds good to me.' Jacob grinned again. 'I can't wait to tell Tabs.'

'Do I look all right?' Rebecca appraised herself in front of the mirror in the Ladies', where about a dozen girls were vying for space to reapply mascara, lipstick and eyeliner.

'Fantastic. Now let's get out there on the pull.' Hannah dragged her friend, laughing, by the hand, back out into the throng at Stefan's thirtieth birthday party. Hannah had been Stefan's neighbour when they were teenagers and they had hung out together. Since her invitation had said Hannah plus one, and she had no current boyfriend, she'd decided Rebecca could do with a night out, especially after that git Ethan had been immutable about not letting her buy out his share of the flat, now that it was already in the hands of the lawyers. Rebecca needed perking up.

Stefan's party was bound to be full of young, eligible men. Hannah knew Rebecca wasn't interested in a relationship, since she was still trying to disengage herself from the mess of the previous one, but a snog with a random stranger at Christmas could only lift your spirits and Rebecca was an extremely pretty girl, even if she didn't know it. She was bound to attract some male attention.

They weaved their way back to the bar. Standing with his back to Rebecca was Ethan. She'd know the set of those shoulders anywhere, plus he was wearing the purple-and-white shirt she'd bought him for his birthday. Just as well she could tell him from the back, as his face was almost completely covered by the blonde locks of a Lycra-clad woman who definitely wasn't just a platonic friend.

Rebecca stopped dead. She couldn't move. They had just split up for God's sake. He'd moved on quickly enough. The girl eventually disentangled herself from Ethan, saw Rebecca standing stock-still in front of her and said, 'Christ, she's stalking us now, Ethan.'

Ethan mumbled something which sounded like 'Sorry?' and turned around. The colour drained from his face when he saw Rebecca and in that moment she knew. He had been right when he said they wanted different things, or in his case different people, one person in particular. He'd told her there was no-one else, but he had lied. It was all becoming clear to her now. This celebrity wannabe whom he'd been wrapped around, was so far from being her, it was risible. What had she said? 'She's stalking us now.' So, they were a couple, and from her comment it appeared not a recent development either.

Through gritted teeth, Rebecca ignored her perma-tanned replacement and, turning to Ethan, said, 'How long?'

Avoiding her eyes, Ethan said, 'I don't know what you mean.'

'Don't insult me any further, Ethan. You owe me that. How long has it been going on? I know you were with her when we were still together. How long?'

Seeing the determined set of Rebecca's jaw, he said in a low voice, 'Seven months.'

'Thanks. That's all I wanted to know. You're perfect for each other, by the way.' She turned on her heel and left, Hannah following close behind her.

'Oh God, Becks, I'm so sorry. I had no idea he knew Stefan.'

'It doesn't matter. Jesus, she could have been Jordan's twin sister. What is it with men?' Then Rebecca burst into tears.

Chapter Twenty-four

23 December

Rebecca's weekend had been spent in a drunken haze, mainly accompanied by Hannah, who felt responsible, although Rebecca kept telling her not to be daft. On Monday morning she still had a stonking sore head, self-inflicted, of course, but she'd blame Ethan for it anyway. She remembered leaving an irate voice message on Ethan's mobile, containing as many expletives as she could fit in. So much for maintaining her dignity, but that's what a quarter bottle of Jägermeister will do to you.

She was dreading the conversation with Henry, who she expected would be very upset at her imminent departure. At least he would know it was purely career advancement which had torn her away. She loved working for him. There were simply no prospects for career progression.

Everyone was busy at Sugar and Spice, as Jacob had roped in Tabitha, too. Well, she may as well do something useful whilst she was there, he said. She had virtually taken up residence in the bakery, reading and sipping lattes, whilst Jacob and Natalie worked. Now she was measuring sugar and butter into the much lusted over BakeMaster 2000 food mixer, as Natalie folded flour into her sponge mix and Jacob managed the front of the shop. With a sense of excitement, Jacob daydreamed of the changes he would like to make when he became manager. He hoped Mrs Williams would allow them, but he already had a vision of a bakery-cum-café-cum-bookshop.

The morning had been quieter than expected; he guessed most people were holding off until the afternoon. The cynical side of Jacob thought this was so they wouldn't have to pay, but the generous side thought they were doing some last-minute Christmas shopping in the morning.

Trestle tables had been set up so it would be easier for patrons to sample the goodies Natalie and Tabitha were preparing. Tabitha had suggested they listen to Radio 1 and whichever Christmas classics they were playing, to get them in the party mood.

Party mood? thought Jacob. *We've had it since the Christmas season began.*

As well as her entire repertoire of Christmas cakes from around the world, Natalie had baked snowmen with white icing and black jelly tots for buttons; reindeer with cinnamon-flavoured ears, chocolate sponge bodies and a cherry for their noses, and carol singers with maple syrup-flavoured halos. The arrangement of novelty cakes would easily entice the public in, placed as they were in the shop window; they were hard to miss.

It wasn't long before the café was filling up in anticipation of the party starting. The savvy clientele and the regulars had the intelligence to show up a bit earlier than the one o'clock start, grab a table, and not move from it, even to go to the toilet, for fear someone might steal their place. They didn't mind parting with the one pound fifty for a cup of tea. Many would be staying at the party until it finished, whereas others would only be able to nip in during their lunch hour and enjoy what little they could.

Rebecca was one of the first to arrive, although it turned out she hadn't known about the party. She told Jacob and Natalie she'd just handed in her notice and that as she'd expected, her boss was gutted, but delighted for her. He was a sweet man and Rebecca hoped that she would be as happy at The Melbourne Gallery. She had been a little bit emotional, said a lot had happened over the past few days, including her giving her ex-boyfriend what for, especially when she met him and his new girlfriend in a club together. She didn't elaborate further, but Jacob got the impression it had not been a satisfactory encounter.

As Natalie and Tabitha busied themselves taking cakes and sausage rolls out of the ovens, Jacob asked Rebecca what she was up to over the next few days.

'I've an appointment with a letting agent tonight at six, to sign a lease for a soulless new-build property which costs the earth,' then realising where she was and that a party was about to start, she said, 'Sorry, just a bit out of sorts today. I'm going to miss my boss, Henry, who's lovely and I feel bad for letting him down. That, on top of having to face up to the fact I'm losing my flat has been a wee bit too much.'

'No need to apologise,' Jacob assured her. 'It's no wonder you're fed up.'

Meanwhile a thought had begun to germinate in Jacob's mind.

Just then a group of people entered the café, laughing and asking if the party had started.

'Yes, in you come, take a seat,' Jacob welcomed them, as he smiled at Rebecca. 'You better grab one yourself if you plan on staying. I reckon it will get busier in here in no time.'

'I think you're right, and thanks for listening to me droning on and on.'

'Don't be silly, that's what friends are for,' said Jacob.

As Rebecca sat down at a corner table, it occurred to her she might have made a mistake turning Jacob down. He really was a gem and good-looking, too. But no, she had done the right thing. The timing was wrong. He couldn't be her rebound guy. He was too good for that, but who knew what might happen in the future.

Natalie passed Jacob carrying cake stands featuring a whole host of heavenly offerings, iced to perfection. They wouldn't have looked out of place on *The Great British Bake Off*. She mingled with the early partygoers, making suggestions in keeping with their tastes and signalled to Tabitha which drinks to bring over, including a non-alcoholic fruit punch and a non-alcoholic Glühwein.

Returning to the kitchen to ensure her latest batch didn't burn, Natalie was waylaid by Jacob.

'You know when you leave in a few days?'

'Yes?'

'What's going to happen to Rose Cottage?'

'I don't know. Mrs Williams hasn't had time to find a tenant yet. She's been too poorly to let it bother her.'

'And it's a nice place?'

'Oh yes, quaint and traditional, but it's all been done up inside, so modern, too.'

'Right.'

'Why?' Natalie asked, curious.

'Nothing, just thinking about something. Could you give me Mrs Williams' number?'

'It's by the phone.' She drew his attention to a number scrawled haphazardly on a piece of paper secured to the wall by a drawing pin.

'Great. Do you mind if I make a quick call?'

'Not at all, but I suggest you keep it short.' Her head inclined towards the door, which had just pinged the arrival of another five or six people, wiping their feet on the mat and starting to take off their coats, as their eyes cast around for a free table.

Jacob was beginning to think Mrs Williams wasn't in when a voice said, 'Hello? Winstanton 420620.'

He always found it endearing that older people tended to answer the phone this way. Soon his generation would only have mobile phones, so they would never do that, as the number would be way too long. It was definitely a generational thing. His father, on the odd occasion he was home, did the same.

'Mrs Williams, this is Jacob from the bakery.'

'Oh hello, dear. Is everything OK?'

'Yes, everything's great. More importantly, how are you feeling?'

'Still a bit achy, dear, if I'm honest, but better than I was a few weeks ago.'

'Well, I'm glad to hear you're getting better. The reason I was phoning is I wondered if you had a tenant for Rose Cottage yet.'

'Oh no, dear, I haven't had a minute to think about that.'

'Well, I have a friend who's interested in moving. I haven't mentioned Rose Cottage to her yet, but I thought I could ask you for the rent costs, things like that, so I can pass the details on to her.'

Jacob chewed his lip as Mrs Williams relayed to him

the information for Rose Cottage.

'That's great, Mrs Williams. If my friend's interested either she or I will call you back. Take care of yourself. Got to go and deal with the customers.'

'Oh yes, it's the party today. How's it going?'

Jacob inspected the scene in front of him. 'Let's just say it's already standing room only.'

'Right, dear. Well, you go and help Natalie.'

'I will, and Mrs Williams?'

'Yes?'

'Thanks for trusting me with your bakery. I won't let you down.'

'I know you won't. Natalie and the customers have told me great things about you. Bye, Jacob.'

He said goodbye, hung up and returned to the front of the bakery, where laughter could be heard and the music had been turned up just a smidge, at the special request of one of the customers, who loved 'Rockin' Around The Christmas Tree'.

Jacob had no possibility to talk to Rebecca straightaway, as the door opened again and a group of young mums with toddlers entered. Wondering where they were going to put their buggies, Jacob was relieved to see they'd felt it safe enough to leave them under the shop awning, where they could keep an eye on them through the window. The toddlers were either on their mums' hips, in their arms, or being towed by the reins.

Once the queue had dissipated, Jacob made a move towards Rebecca. He didn't want to miss her leaving and her in turn, miss out on Rose Cottage, which he thought could be just what she was looking for.

'Rebecca,' he interrupted her talking to an old lady who had asked if she could share her table. 'Sorry to disturb you, but have you got a second? I think I might have an answer to your flat problem,' he said.

Rebecca's face lit up. 'Really?'

'Really!' Jacob grinned, and he told her all about Rose Cottage, how he'd already asked Mrs Williams about the cost and the lease conditions, in case she was interested.

'You're a treasure,' she said, standing up and kissing him on the cheek. 'I really appreciate it. Can I see it?'

Jacob explained that Natalie was currently living in it, but why didn't she ask her if she could view it.

Sophie entered the bakery just then with Meredith. Her happy expression turned to one of sadness for an instant, then she quickly planted a fake smile on her face, when Meredith turned to her and said, 'Look at the tree, it's almost iridescent, from all those baubles.'

'Hello, Meredith, how are you feeling? It's lovely to see you up and about.'

'Much better, thanks. Not well enough to drive myself around yet, but hopefully after New Year. I won't be back at work until at least the middle of the month, though. Doctor's orders.'

'I'm glad you're listening to them,' Natalie said, clasping Meredith's black-gloved hand in hers. 'So good to see you up and about again.'

'Thank you.'

'Right, where can we sit you?'

Natalie asked a young couple if they would mind sharing a table with Sophie and Meredith. They were happy to, but explained they had to leave in five minutes, anyway.

Now that Natalie was free again, Rebecca saw her opportunity. 'Natalie?'

'Yes, Rebecca? Enjoying yourself?' she asked, as she topped up the trestle table with *marquesas*.

'Yes, thanks. What are those?' Her curiosity got the better of her.

'Spanish Christmas sponge cakes made with almonds and lemons.'

'Mmm, sounds delicious.' Rebecca practically salivated, even though she'd had two small cakes already.

'Try one,' urged Natalie. 'You'll enjoy it, I promise.'

Rebecca regarded her waistband and bit her lip. 'I'm not sure if I'll still be comfortable in these trousers if I eat another.'

Natalie laughed, then said, 'Take it home, then.'

'Interesting you should say home, that's exactly why I wanted to speak to you.' She then explained to Natalie about her housing situation.

'Give me just a second.' Natalie went through the back and picked up her bag. 'Here are the keys. Sorry it's not as tidy as I would have liked if I'd known anyone would be viewing it, but here, I don't need them back until five.'

'Are you sure?'

'Absolutely. You have an honest face,' she replied. 'And I have nothing worth stealing,' she joked.

'Thanks ever so much.' Rebecca was elated.

Natalie put the cake in a bag for her and said, 'Don't forget this, and feel free to have a cup of tea when you're there, take in your surroundings properly.'

Rebecca shot her a huge smile and waved goodbye to Jacob as she left.

Jacob was circulating, ensuring each table had enough drinks and that their cake stands were replenished. He also topped up the trestle tables with supplies.

'Hi, I didn't see you two come in. How are you, Meredith?' Jacob asked politely.

'Feeling much better, thanks, and thank you again for calling the ambulance.'

'You're welcome. Anyone would have done the same.'

'Nonetheless, I wanted to thank you.'

Jacob acknowledged her continued thanks by a slight raise of his head, then he turned to Sophie and asked her how she was doing.

'Not bad,' she said, not quite meeting his eye.

'What do you think of the cakes?' Jacob asked, wondering why he had the feeling something was amiss.

'Lovely, especially the coconut one.' Sophie took a bite, which rendered her unable to say any more.

'That's lamington, an Australian cake. Strictly speaking it's not just a Christmas cake, the Aussies eat it at other times, too, but Natalie wanted to include it. I can see why.'

'Mmm,' said Sophie, enjoying another mouthful.

'Well, I'll leave you girls to it, must offload these.' Jacob moved off with his cake stands.

'Do you want to tell me what's going on?' Meredith asked Sophie.

'Sorry?'

'With you and Brad Pitt there.'

'He looks nothing like Brad Pitt.'

'He does, well, a younger Brad Pitt, but let's not split hairs,' Meredith went on.

Sophie realised this was the first conversation remotely resembling a girly chat she had ever had with Meredith. Funnily enough, the thought no longer unsettled her, apart from for the obvious reason that she didn't want to talk about Jacob.

'So what's going on between you two?'

'Nothing.' Sophie found the tassel on her handbag scintillating, all of a sudden.

'Don't give me that,' Meredith said, not unkindly. 'There's definitely something going on between you.'

Knowing that Meredith was tenacious as hell, Sophie caved in. 'Nothing's going on between us, seriously. Anyway, he has a girlfriend.'

'Are you sure?' Meredith's eyes bored into Sophie's.

'She was in earlier. You must have seen her; beautiful, with fiery red hair, a bit like a Renaissance Madonna.'

'As opposed to the pop star with conical underwear?' Meredith made an attempt at humour. 'Are you sure?'

'Yes,' Sophie replied, her voice flat. 'I saw her kissing him earlier.'

'Hmm, well that puts paid to that then. I'm guessing you're not the type to go after another girl's man.'

'Correct.'

'Well, in that case, bad luck. Why don't we drown your sorrows with some alcohol-free *Gluhwein*?' Meredith raised her glass.

'Oh, what a beautiful tree,' Catherine exclaimed when they were barely in the door. They were lucky to get in the door; the bakery was absolutely heaving.

Stanley oohed and aahed at the glittery and unusual baubles on the tree. He, too, had ordered a tree once he knew Thomas and Catherine were coming, as he didn't want to greet them in a house devoid of festive atmosphere, particularly as they had chosen this season to get married. But his tree bore no resemblance to this vision before him, which looked truly magical. He felt silly thinking this, but he could just feel the goodwill in the air, in this room, with these people; he was starting to look forward to Christmas.

Natalie came forward to greet them and Stanley proudly presented his grandson and granddaughter-to-be. What a mouthful that was, he thought. Next time he would just say granddaughter. Natalie wanted all the details of the wedding, and congratulated the happy couple on having chosen such a fantastic venue, particularly with all the snow on the ground, their big day was bound to be spectacular and their wedding photographs amazing.

Meredith saw her chance, whilst Natalie was otherwise engaged. Gesturing with her empty glass she said, 'Actually this Glühwein without the wine in it is quite good, I'm going to get another. Do you want one?'

'Yes, please, it is pretty nice, isn't it?' Sophie said.

Meredith nodded, then made her way through the crowds of people, who were now milling around, holding sausage rolls and glasses of non-alcoholic punch, since there were no seats left.

'Me again,' she said to Jacob. 'That Glühwein really does make you feel Christmassy.'

Jacob agreed that it did and said, 'And because it's non-alcoholic, Natalie and I can have some, too!'

'Win-win!' Meredith declared. She was behaving slightly drunk, although that wasn't possible. Maybe it was the medication which had sent her a bit loopy, making her want to be Winstanton's matchmaker. She'd never been one for letting opportunities pass her by and she was damned if she was going to let Sophie. Now to find out for sure.

'So, are you doing anything nice for Christmas?' It was lame, but fail-safe, Christmas being only a few days away.

'I'm spending it with my sister, Tabitha.' He inclined

his head towards a girl sitting chatting to an elderly man and a young couple, her interest in what they were saying clear, from the way she was leaning in to listen to them. Meredith noticed she had a barely visible bump, but was definitely pregnant. For one who had a sister with four children, she knew the signs.

'Oh, that sounds nice. Are you cooking?'

'God, no! I'm a terrible cook. Thankfully Tabitha's brilliant.' Jacob went on to outline what they were having for Christmas dinner.

'Mmm, you're making my mouth water,' Meredith told him. 'So your girlfriend isn't joining you for Christmas dinner?'

Giving her a strange look, Jacob said, 'No.'

'Spending it with her own family, is she?' Meredith wouldn't let it go.

Hesitating, Jacob finally mumbled, 'Erm, I'm between girlfriends.'

'Really?'

Looking uncomfortable, Jacob handed Meredith the two Glühweins. She thanked him, wished him Merry Christmas and returned to Sophie, but not before she saw the confused expression on Jacob's face.

'She's not his girlfriend. He doesn't have one.' Meredith came right out and said it.

'You didn't ask him.' Sophie's eyes widened in horror.

'What do you take me for? I was far more subtle than that.' Meredith stretched the truth. 'He's spending Christmas with his sister.'

'The pregnant one?' Sophie glanced over at Tabitha, who was happily munching away on cake, taking a much-deserved rest from assisting Natalie.

'Yep.'

'Well, he may be unattached, but that doesn't change matters. He obviously has a thing for the girl with the red hair and Botticelli curls.'

Meredith smiled a knowing smile.

Once he'd topped drinks up again, distributed cakes and made small talk, Jacob paused to draw breath and wipe his perspiring brow with a handkerchief. Natalie sidled up to him. 'It's going well, isn't it?'

'Better than I thought. I was just thinking, we need to get some business cards printed, so people who come in can pass them on to friends.'

'Good idea. Well, you'll be the boss in a few days. That can be one of your first tasks.'

Jacob was only half listening to Natalie and blushed as she turned to see what had captured his attention.

'Ah, yes, it's good to see Meredith back on her feet, glad she's well enough to enjoy Christmas.'

'Hmm.'

'What's up?' Natalie pressed him.

'Nothing,' he lied.

'C'mon. We've been working almost on top of each other for three weeks now. I know something's up.'

'Well,' confided Jacob, uncomfortable at discussing it, 'I think Meredith was flirting with me earlier. She was asking me about my girlfriend.'

Natalie stared at him, then said, 'Jacob, sometimes men can be very dim. Look at Meredith now. What do you see?'

Reluctantly and hoping they didn't make eye contact, as God knows what she'd think then, Jacob glanced over to where Meredith was sitting. 'She's talking to Sophie,' he said, unable to think of any other clue which the tableau offered him.

'Bingo.'

Jacob still didn't get it.

'Jacob, do you really think a woman in her forties is likely to be interested in you, or do you think there's a much more plausible explanation?'

The cells in Jacob's brain put in some overtime and *Eureka!* 'Sophie?'

Natalie clapped her hands together in applause, winked at him and then turned to speak to a customer who had approached the counter.

Jacob looked over at Meredith and Sophie. He liked Sophie. She was nice, more than nice, funny, clearly clever, since she was almost single-handedly running Meredith's company at the moment, and, now he looked at her properly, he saw she was very pretty, in a completely different way to Rebecca. He'd been so busy obsessing over Rebecca, he hadn't noticed what was right in front of him.

As the party drew to a close, Meredith and Sophie stood to leave. Terrified, but determined not to let the opportunity pass him by, Jacob approached them and said, 'Sophie, have you got a minute?'

'Sure.' She stepped aside to let Stanley, Thomas and Catherine pass, as they waved goodbye to Natalie and promised they'd be in again before New Year.

'I know it's short notice, but I was wondering if you had anything on tonight.'

A wide smile radiated across Sophie's face, as she said with delight, 'No, just some present wrapping in the company of a bottle of wine.'

'Well, in that case, would you like to have a glass of wine, or two, with me tonight?'

Sophie's cheeks turned scarlet, then she said, 'I'd like that a lot.'

Jacob thought on his feet and proposed they meet in the Crooked Dug pub at eight o'clock.

As Sophie returned to Meredith, who was clearly grilling her on the way out, Tabitha and Natalie shared a complicit look. Love was in the air.

Chapter Twenty-five

Christmas Eve

These shoes are a nightmare to put on, Stanley thought, as he tried to lace up his dress kilt shoes. It was no good. He'd have to ask someone to help him when he got to the church and just wear his normal shoes on the way there. Surveying himself in the mirror, he was surprised by what he saw. He looked quite handsome, if considerably older than last time he'd worn his kilt. Since his family name had no tartan, many years ago he'd shortlisted those he liked best, before selecting the Brodie modern tartan; red and black with thin yellow stripes. It wasn't as bold as the Leslie tartan, but he preferred the understated look. He thought it suited him and thankfully it still fitted him, although he needed to pull the belt in two more notches than before.

Jacob arrived at the bakery ten minutes later than usual, mumbling apologies to Natalie as he removed his jacket, the huge grin on his face indicative of how his date with Sophie had gone the night before.

'Well, there's no point asking how you got on last night!' Natalie said to him as she poured him a coffee.

'Fantastic. She's so–' he searched for the correct word

to use '–right for me. We get each other. We talked until we got thrown out of the pub, because it was closing time. And get this, Meredith has promoted her and given her a massive Christmas bonus, too. Sophie was like a dog with two tails.' Jacob finally drew breath.

Natalie hid a smile. She knew quite well why Sophie had been so overjoyed and it had nothing to do with work, delighted though she might be about her improved career prospects and burgeoning bank balance. Very little got past Natalie; it was her job to know about people and ever since day one, when they had first met Sophie, she'd known that there was a spark between her and Jacob. It had just taken Jacob a little while to notice. Men could be so oblivious.

The bakery was just as busy today as it had been the day before. Their marketing efforts had worked. Spreading Christmas cheer had the till ringing non-stop, as anxious holidaymakers made their final purchases, then relaxed with a hot chocolate and a slice of cake. Although a few tense-looking husbands were being trailed along by purposeful wives, laden down with bags of toys and other gifts, generally the atmosphere was one of excitement and happiness. Christmas Eve – the most magical night of the year.

The door jangled once more and Rebecca blew in, a whirlwind of energy, and bestowed her biggest smile on Jacob.

'Thanks so much. I've just been to see Mrs Williams and I can move into Rose Cottage after New Year. It's beautiful, too, so quirky and picturesque. It suits my artistic side.'

'I'm really pleased it's all working out for you.' Jacob

patted her arm. Rebecca felt a tingle surge through her. Yet when she looked up at him, his expression was different to how he'd been with her before. He didn't look sorrowful, as if he was wistful for what might have been. No, he seemed...content, happy. Whatever had happened? She decided that she was happy for him. He was a lovely guy and yes, perhaps they would have been good together, but timing was everything and it hadn't been right for them.

'Right, I better get on. I have a train to catch,' she said, glancing at her watch.

'Oh, where are you off to?'

'Banbury.'

Seeing Jacob's eyebrow shoot up, Rebecca explained, 'My parents moved there a few years ago. I'm spending Christmas with them.'

As the words left her mouth, Rebecca realised she was no longer dreading the visit. She could cope with the grilling her mother would no doubt make her endure, safe in the knowledge that in a few days' time she would be heading home again, soon to start her new job and move into Rose Cottage.

As Catherine and her uncle, taking the place of her long-dead father, walked down the aisle towards the waiting groom, Stanley sat in the front row reserved for relatives. Tears coursed down his face. He hadn't expected to see this moment and how he wished Edie were here beside him. He could feel her presence now, scolding him, telling him that at least one of them was able to witness it and that he should rejoice in the occasion.

Whilst the two young people exchanged the vows they had written themselves, hands intertwined, Stanley cast his mind back to his own wedding, in this very church, all those years before, and he was thankful that history was repeating itself. He only hoped the newlyweds would experience as much happiness as he and Edie had in the many years they had spent together.

At two o'clock on the banks of Loch Lomond, freezing to death almost, but cheerful nonetheless, the wedding party posed for photographs. They had been lucky with the weather. Although the temperature was below zero, fluffy white clouds buzzed across a predominantly blue sky, and not a drop of rain had fallen. Stanley was glad of his Bonnie Prince Charlie jacket, his woollen kilt and knee-high kilt socks. The shoes, though, were almost paper-thin and he could barely feel his toes. Judging that he had enough decent shots now, the photographer deemed that they could all repair to the warmth of the hotel, where the reception was soon to take place.

As Natalie closed the bakery for the final time, she remembered the lovely comments customers had made to her when they discovered today would be her last. She had shed a silent tear, even though this was always the way. Tabitha sat on a chair, rubbing her stomach, whether she had overindulged, or if she was bonding with her unborn child, it was hard to tell.

'Well, this is us,' said Natalie.

'I can't believe we won't see you again,' said Jacob. 'I feel as if I've known you much longer than three weeks.'

'I know. That's the sign of good friends,' said Natalie. 'I'm glad I met you, Jacob.'

'Me too.' Jacob's voice cracked and he stuck his hands in his pockets.

'And you.' Natalie turned her affectionate gaze on Tabitha.

'Thanks, you too. And thanks for looking after my brother.'

'Oh, it was nothing. Just you take care of that baby. I'll keep in touch so I know how it all goes.'

'I'd like that,' said Tabitha, hugging her.

'Before I forget, I have a little something for both of you under the tree,' Natalie said.

'So do I,' said Jacob.

They both retrieved the presents from under the tree.

'Oh, but what about your baubles and decorations?' Jacob asked. 'How will we get them back to you?'

'Oh, don't worry, Mrs Williams knows how to return them to me,' Natalie assured him.

Jacob exhaled. 'That's a relief. For a second I'd envisaged us dismantling the tree tonight, before the main event.'

Natalie laughed. 'I wouldn't do that to you. Here, Tabitha, why don't you open yours first?' Natalie held out a foil-wrapped package to her. The packaging shone as if illuminated from the inside. Carefully Tabitha unwrapped the parcel.

'Sorry, I know I'm slow, but I love the anticipation of presents as much as I love the presents themselves,' Tabitha apologised.

Natalie smiled at her and continued to do so as Tabitha gasped at the antique silver-and-mother-of-pearl baby rattle which lay in a navy velvet box.

'Oh, this is too much, Natalie. It's beautiful. It looks so old.'

'It is,' Natalie confirmed without elaborating further.

'It's beautiful,' Tabitha repeated, mesmerised. 'Look, Jacob.'

Turning it over and over in his hand, Jacob agreed that

it was exquisite.

'Now you, Natalie. This is from myself and Tabitha,' said Jacob, as he presented her with a small gold-coloured gift bag. Natalie noticed it was very light. Opening it, she saw that nestling within was a Christmas bauble, in a blue-and-white mosaic style, depicting the Nativity.

'This is amazing.' Natalie was touched. 'What a thoughtful gift. I shall hang it every year with the others. Thank you so much.' She kissed them both on the cheeks.

Then, it was Jacob's turn, as Natalie passed him a black leather box. Inside lay a snow globe. Surprised, and unsure what to say, although he was wondering why Natalie had bought him a snow globe, he examined the unusually heavy snow globe; more akin in weight to a paperweight. As he took in the tableau it featured, he discovered he was seeing High St, where the bakery was situated. Yep, and there was the bakery, complete with the tip of the Christmas tree visible through the window.

'But how did you...? This is...unbelievable.' Jacob stared at it. For a second he though he saw something move, but it must have been his vision blurring. He could have sworn he saw movement outside the butcher shop two doors up. As he glanced at Natalie, she was smiling at him. Just then he saw Pat, the butcher, walk past the shop window. Jacob shook his head. What a weird coincidence.

'I love it,' he told Natalie. 'I still don't know how you got someone to make you one with our row of shops in it, but it's brilliant. Thank you.' He wrapped her in a bear hug.

Natalie shone with pleasure. 'I hope after I've gone, you'll occasionally look at it and remember me.'

'Oh, you can count on it.'

After several more hugs and after wishing each other

Merry Christmas, they parted ways outside the shop, promising to keep in touch.

As Natalie returned to Rose Cottage, she thought, *Almost done*, and she couldn't help feeling a little wistful.

'Mummy, I don't want to go to bed yet,' a sleepy Max said, sucking his thumb and pulling on his beige floppy-eared rabbit – well, one-eared, he'd chewed the other one off over time.

'But Santa won't come if you're not asleep,' Amelia reasoned with him.

Eleven-year-old Alannah, fresh and rosy-cheeked from her bath, sat between Meredith's knees whilst her aunt combed her long blonde hair. Seven-year-old Edward lay on his stomach, face in his hands, resting on his elbows, as the whole family watched *The Grinch*. The children all wore new pyjamas; Santa ones for Max, reindeer covered Edward's, and a red onesie populated with snowmen and snowflakes for Alannah. Jasper was the only one who didn't participate in this ritual.

Curling up on his mum's lap, Max said, 'OK, but I want to leave the milk for Santa.'

'That's fine.' Amelia ruffled his hair.

'And biscuits, too,' Alannah said, jumping to her feet. 'I'll be back, Auntie Meredith, once we've sorted the biscuits for Santa.' She winked at her. As Alannah walked off holding her little brother's hand, Meredith heard Edward say, 'And we need carrots for the reindeer, Mummy. They have such a long journey – they must get very tired.'

'Shit,' said Gareth, hoisting himself out of the armchair. 'I was meant to fetch some carrots from the garden for the damned reindeer. Jasper, do you know where the torch is?'

'In the utility room, Dad. I'll get the carrots if you

want,' he offered.

'No, it's all right. Can you just pause the TV for me, please?'

Jasper and Meredith sat in companionable silence until Gareth returned a few minutes later.

Meredith was admiring her surroundings. This really was a happy home. The scent of pine from the tree was powerful, heady and welcoming. No-one minded the occasional 'Ouch' from standing on the needles, although the living room had been vacuumed every day since the tree's arrival. There was barely room to move near the tree. In fact, everyone had to leave the living room by circumventing the tree, there were so many presents under it and around it; and those were just the presents from each other, not the big presents from Santa.

Although Meredith believed kids got too much these days, for once she said nothing and sat back with a glass of red wine, which Gareth had brought her on his return, saying, 'I'm sure one won't hurt,' and enjoyed the family scene. She'd never spent Christmas Eve with children before and had been infected by their enthusiasm and excitement. Edward had been the opposite to Max; he had wanted to go to bed at six thirty, as he thought the earlier he went to bed, the sooner Santa would arrive. Since his parents didn't want him getting up at two o'clock, his mum had told him he could go in a few hours, at the usual time.

After ensuring final preparations for the following day's dinner were taken care of, Amelia joined her family to watch *The Grinch*. They'd seen it so many times, but it had become customary to watch it on Christmas Eve. Meredith watched her sister take in the scene in front of the fire – Amelia's house sported an original coal fire, not one of those pretend living-flame ones – children, dog, semi-snoozing husband, and then her gaze fell on Meredith. Their eyes met and no words were needed between the sisters to convey how glad they were to be spending Christmas together.

'It's so good to see you, darling.' Rebecca's father hugged her, almost lifting her off her feet, as they stood together on the platform at Banbury Station. He'd come to pick her up, even though she'd said she would call a taxi. 'Nonsense', he'd said, 'it's no trouble at all.' Plus he'd waited too long to see her already. What he really meant was he wanted a chat with his daughter, a friendly one, without her mother, and for that Rebecca was grateful. She'd always been close to her father, less so her mum, who meant well, but was very opinionated and as stubborn as they came. As she returned her father's embrace, Rebecca felt glad she'd made the effort. Christmas was for families, for better or worse.

Chapter Twenty-six

Christmas Day

Meredith awoke to shouts of 'Santa's been, Mummy, Santa's been.' She was pretty sure she recognised the owner of the voice as Edward. Smiling as she dropped her legs over the side of the bed, she thought back to when she was his age and Christmas had still held that sense of wonder. Her presents had included a doctor's kit and the most beautiful doll's house she had ever seen. No-one knew this, but she still had it in her attic.

She cleaned her teeth, threw on her dressing gown and traipsed downstairs. She was last down. Jasper and Alannah were at the front of the tree, passing presents back to everyone. Edward and Max were given most of their presents before the others. Edward tore the wrapping paper off his first present, uncovering an Avengers Assemble figure: Thor. Alannah helped Max remove a Peppa Pig space rocket from his parcel, to shrieks of delight and exclamations of *'Look Mummy, Peppa!'* Amelia didn't need to feign enthusiasm; the expression on her son's face was all she needed to exude genuine pleasure.

The children's presents were torn open, marvelled at, and wrapping paper discarded, as the next gift arrived on their lap or into their outstretched hands. Gareth went around picking up all the abandoned gift wrap, stuffing it unceremoniously into a bin bag he'd fetched from the kitchen. There, they could see the floor again, and the rest of the presents. There was nothing worse than a new toy being trodden on and broken or damaged because someone hadn't seen it for the carnage that was their living room on Christmas morning, Gareth told Meredith. One of Edward's train carriages had gone that way the year before, so Gareth had learned his lesson.

In between hugs and kisses and cries of *Thank you, Mummy, thank you, Daddy*, Amelia and Gareth moved the previous toy to the side of the relevant child. Each child had their own corner of the room where they could place their gifts. The children had their own rooms and a playroom, but Christmas Day was sacred in Amelia's house, and they were pretty much allowed to do what they wanted. Christmas was all about the children. Mess and chaos reigned and that was the way it should be. Gareth explained that his role was to assemble everything that required it. Already he was pulling the cable ties off boxes and trying to get inside, so he could insert batteries, ever mindful of a patiently waiting child who wanted to play with it.

Meredith heard Gareth curse the toy manufacturers under his breath – *Who packaged these things?* They were a nightmare to get into, as if the manufacturers were having a good old laugh at the expense of the parents.

Unable to contain himself any longer, Max dived on another present which had been given to him, and asked his mum to help him open it. She was helping Edward, so Meredith suggested she do it for him. Paper removed, it revealed a Bananas in Pyjamas funhouse, which was met with whoops of glee from Max, who was literally bouncing on the spot. The funhouse involved no assembly and had packaging that hadn't been put together by a contortionist, so after Meredith had inserted two AA batteries, Max was soon playing with his funhouse whilst his older siblings took a few minutes to open their gifts. An iPad Mini had Jasper grinning from ear to ear, and Alannah's digital camera with integrated video camera provoked squeals of joy. The children continued to open their gifts, exclaiming in wonder at many of them, each having a bigger wow factor than the last.

Soon the children had opened all their presents, and the younger ones began to play with their toys, as Alannah and Jasper passed gifts to their parents and aunt. Meredith loved the cashmere jumper Amelia and Gareth had bought her. Max had wrapped a gift for her, which turned out to be his Mr Matey bubble bath. She was touched that he had thought of her, and promised to use it that night, and she meant it. She might be much more accustomed to Crème de la Mer products, but her beloved youngest nephew had donated his much-cherished bubble bath, so she was determined to use and enjoy it. Mr Matey – she couldn't believe he was still around. That was one of the gifts their parents had bought them every year. Clearly Amelia had continued the tradition.

As Amelia instructed the children to make some space, so they could play with their toys, Gareth said he was off to make bacon rolls. It was now six o'clock and Christmas lunch was still a long way off. Meredith offered to help, and as she passed Edward and Max, playing happily together, showing each other their new toys and finding each other's toys even more interesting than those they had received themselves, Meredith felt privileged to be a part of their Christmas.

'Merry Christmas, everyone.' Sophie's father raised a glass of pink champagne to his daughters and wife.

'Merry Christmas, Dad,' 'Merry Christmas, darling,' came the replies as they chinked glasses together.

Sophie's family had arisen at the much more respectable time of nine o'clock, with her parents waking the girls only at ten o'clock. Sophie hadn't slept much. Jacob had been populating her dreams, awake and asleep. She had lain for hours the night before reliving their evening together. He'd finally kissed her when he walked her home and it had been everything she had expected and more. Warm, inviting, sexy, she couldn't wait until the next one. Fortunately she didn't have much longer to wait. He'd asked her if she wanted to meet up on Boxing Night, so she had precisely thirty-four more hours to go. She hadn't told her family yet, not even her sisters, to whom she was very close. She didn't want to jinx things. For now she hugged the secret to herself and said, yes, she would like a cup of tea, when her sister asked her for the third time.

As she opened her presents with her family, she tried to keep her mind on the day. But Christmas had come a day early for Sophie, and she couldn't be happier.

Stanley's routine didn't change on Christmas morning. The wedding reception had lasted well into the wee small hours and it was gone two o'clock by the time the taxi dropped him home. He'd hung up his dress clothes, so they could air, gone through his usual ablutions, then gone to bed. He'd decided he would tell Edie all about the wedding in the morning.

At half past six, Stanley was up once more. Irrespective of what time he went to bed, he woke at the same time:

the curse, or joy, depending on which way you looked at it, of getting old. He made two cups of tea and carried them over to the kitchen table. Sitting down, he picked one up and took a sip. Ah, that was better. He then wished Edie a Merry Christmas and told her about the wedding in as much detail as he could remember. He told her of the guests, the ambiance, the venue, the bride's dress; even though he didn't know anything about styles, cuts and materials, he described it as best he could. He knew if Edie were here with him, she'd be rolling her eyes and telling him he didn't have a clue about fashion.

The sumptuous menu was gone into in great detail, everything from the Loch Etive smoked salmon terrine he'd eaten for starters, to the beef wellington he'd had with fresh roasted asparagus, green beans spritzed with lemon juice and a carrot mash. It had been visually pleasing and hadn't gone unnoticed by his palate either. He'd chosen the more traditional dessert of homemade apple pie and custard, although it had also included pumpkin, which was new to him. He had avoided the sorbet, which had always seemed like an excuse not to serve real ice cream, and panna cotta really didn't sound his kind of thing.

Stanley regaled Edie with tales of the ceilidh and the fun he'd had. Even he had joined in insofar as he was able. He'd declined Strip the Willow, a lethal dance which often ended up in sprained ankles, or someone getting an elbow in the face by accident, and which almost always left its participants covered in bruises. But he'd managed Pride of Erin and a few other waltzes, and had really enjoyed himself, as he'd danced with the bride and a few of the bride's relatives who had flown in from Canada. He recalled when he and Edie had been courting and they had gone to a ceilidh in a hotel in Killin in Perthshire. They'd stayed with relatives of Edie back then, and they had danced to every jig and reel, only finishing, breathless, when the band declared they would be back again the following week, but that was them done for the night. He knew Edie would be thinking of that night, too, and he was warmed by the thought.

Tabitha sat cross-legged whilst she still could, her bump small, but discernible, and passed presents over to Jacob. She had been, as ever, too generous, and Jacob felt bad that he had been able to buy her so little. But she had waved away his protests of 'This is too much,' as well as having ignored his fifty pounds maximum he had set on gifts this year, as he simply didn't have the money. 'Tabs, you've spent at least six times our limit.' Jacob was perplexed.

'Jacob, it's not about the money, it's about the giving,' she told him.

Realising there was truth in this and wondering if his parents had ever thought of it that way when they lavished gifts on them all throughout their childhood to make up for their absence, Jacob relented and decided just to accept his gifts in the spirit they were given.

He'd chosen a few items of maternity clothing for Tabitha. She had been moaning that her tops were starting to get too tight and he'd zoned in on that comment. He was surprisingly good at choosing clothes and knew his sister's tastes well.

Tabitha had ordered most of the food and ingredients from Fortnum & Mason, determined they would have a fabulous Christmas dinner together, since it was just the two of them, although technically she pointed out, there were three of them present. She had some trouble getting her head round that.

Jacob agreed it was odd and a rush of anticipation surged through him. This time next year he'd be an uncle. There would be a baby to contend with, buy gifts for and care for. It would be marvellous. He loved children. And on top of that, he might have a girlfriend. OK, he'd only had one date with Sophie, but he had a good feeling. Next year could turn out to be a pretty exciting one.

Contrary to expectation, Rebecca's mother hadn't subjected her to the third degree on arrival the night before, and in fact Rebecca had spent an enjoyable evening with her parents having a low-key meal and a few glasses of wine, in her case, and sherry in her parents'. So on Christmas morning, she was expecting some throwaway comment from her mum, which would be chock-full of meaning, but it never came, and gradually she felt less and less on edge. By the time the Queen's Speech came on at three o'clock, there was little likelihood of her mother broaching the subject of Ethan and how much she thought he was right for Rebecca. Maybe she had got away with it.

Dinner was a lovely, quiet affair with the TV off and discussion which centred around what there was to do in Oxfordshire, as well as the hot news items Rebecca had brought to the table: her job and her new home. In fact, her mother had been nothing short of helpful, giving advice when asked, as opposed to sticking her oar in where it wasn't wanted, which she was wont to do.

Rebecca surprised herself by discovering she was having a good time; surprise which must have manifested itself in her expression, as her father at one point gave her the thumbs-up sign. It was terrible being the only child a lot of the time. You always had to be there for your parents as they had no-one else to call upon, and whilst Rebecca didn't mean this to sound uncharitable, being the constant focus of your parents' attention could be exhausting sometimes.

Rebecca's father was a mild, understated man who took comfort in the simple things in life. Having his daughter home for Christmas was present enough for him, as he sat in his armchair and watched her relaxing. Never one to cause a fuss, this time he'd stood up for her. When his wife had been hysterical about their darling daughter splitting up from Ethan, for once he had intervened. Rebecca was having a hard enough time of it, having to give up her beloved flat, not to mention having to mend her broken heart. What she didn't need was her mother wading in with her size sixes and making her feel as if no-one was on her side. Rebecca's mother had been so flabbergasted at being addressed in this way that she capitulated. It was rare for her husband to cause a scene or voice opinions contrary to her own, so when he did, she knew he meant it and he wasn't to be trifled with.

As she sat in her parents' cosy living room, watching *Only Fools and Horses* and *Who Wants To Be A Millionaire*'s Christmas episode, eating orange Matchmakers, the occasional leftover After Eight and sipping her glass of Shiraz, Rebecca felt more at peace than she had done for the past year with Ethan.

She thought back to the previous Christmas when she, excited, had got out of bed at ten o'clock, which by Christmas morning standards and by her estimation was pretty late, and brought Ethan a cup of tea and a boiled egg with toast soldiers. He'd once let slip when drunk that it was his guilty pleasure, but that she mustn't tell anyone, as he'd never live it down.

Hungover, Ethan hadn't appreciated the gesture and had rolled over and gone back to sleep, leaving his breakfast untouched. Rebecca, deflated, had gone into the living room and opened a few presents she had received from friends.

But that hadn't been the only time he had shown his true colours, ungrateful prat, and as Rebecca continued to reflect, it struck her that she had been lonely for a long time. She had never thought she would be that person who was lonely in a relationship, but now that it was staring her in the face, she knew that was what she had become and she was glad to be rid of him. Deciding that the five minutes she had spent thinking of him today was four too many, Rebecca picked up the TV guide, flicked through it, then asked if anyone minded if she watched the *Downton Abbey* Christmas special.

Natalie, too, was watching the Queen's Speech and hoping her luck had changed. She'd had a good year this year with the birth of Prince George. Natalie had always admired the queen, second only to Queen Victoria in her opinion, both long-reigning monarchs, with a fair bit of responsibility on their hands, both unlucky in many ways, she always thought, but blessed in others. As she added some more custard to her Christmas pudding, she congratulated herself on a job well done. This year had gone exceptionally well.

Crackers were pulled, party hats were donned, whistles were blown at Aberlomond House Hotel, as Stanley dined with his grandchildren, for he now thought of Catherine as his granddaughter. They were joined by many of the wedding guests and relatives, who had either come from abroad or who had extended their stay to include a Christmas break after the wedding. In total there were nineteen of them. Stanley thought, except for the absence of his beloved wife and son, this could possibly be the best Christmas Day ever. Who knew that having Christmas outside of the home could be so wonderful and such fun.

As Stanley tucked into his posh dinner: ham hough in herb ballatine, pan-seared black gold fillet steak with roast root vegetables and a red wine jus, rounding off with meringue with Chantilly cream and boozy berries, instead of the usual traditional Christmas pudding, Stanley thanked God for the arrival of his grandson.

Catherine and Thomas would soon leave to start their honeymoon up north, and he would see them only on their return trip, before they flew out of Glasgow Airport the day after. Yet, although Stanley knew he would miss them a great deal, he felt buoyed by the new friendships he had made at the club and had been invited round to George's for a small sherry on Boxing Night. Finally there was something he could be grateful for this year, and he now had something to look forward to next year too.

Even in as grand a house as Amelia's, fitting twenty-one people in comfortably for dinner was a tall order. The main dining table, which seated twelve, was sandwiched between two smaller tables; one had been added at each end. The result was haphazard but it worked, although those at the opposite ends of the table had to shout to be heard by the person furthest away. The seven of them, Gareth's parents and his siblings, their children, a couple of Gareth's cousins, Meredith and Amelia's own parents, plus two of the children's friends whose parents were working overseas for Christmas, and a work colleague of Gareth's who was single this year with no family close by, made up the twenty-one. It was quite a haul.

Amelia had prepared everything from scratch, although being good at delegating, unlike Meredith, who was only beginning to learn, had roped in her older children and her husband with the simpler tasks and even Edward had helped set the table. Red festive runners ran the length of the three tables, whilst tasteful centrepieces of silver and gold intertwined snowflakes and Christmas trees adorned each one. The dinner service used on only special occasions had been polished until it shone, as had the crystal glasses. Edward had done a stellar job. When the guests had arrived for pre-lunch drinks at two o'clock, they had been shown into the lounge, not the living room, which was the children's haven on Christmas morning, and although now free of wrapping paper and other detritus, was still bursting with toys, books, clothes and selection boxes.

The lounge also sported a beautiful Scots pine, this covered solely in white lights set on a timer and which had ten different modes. Red-and-white candles in elaborate candelabra, many of them antique, lit the remainder of the room; one of Amelia's passions was to collect certain items – candleholders was one of them. A makeshift bar had been erected at one end of the room and Jasper acted as barman, although his mother did check occasionally to ensure he didn't imbibe. He may be almost of age but she didn't want him falling face down into his Christmas pudding.

Dinner was exceptional and not only the food. The company, Meredith found, was to her liking. She was starting to feel in better health and she was certain much of it was down to the easy way Amelia ran her chaotic household: with lots of love. So, too, her dinner parties were events to which one could aspire. She had to applaud Amelia – she knew how to bring out the best in everyone and every situation. Looking around the table, Meredith saw only beaming smiles, heard only raucous laughter and intermittent giggles. She felt truly honoured to be part of it and hoped there would be many such occasions in the future.

Long after her mother had gone to bed, and that was late as they had played board games for a few hours first, something they hadn't done since she was a child, Rebecca sat cradling a glass of wine and chatting with her father. Too much time had elapsed since they had done this properly – they were still close, but it was never the same over the phone. Normally she would have discussed with her dad at length the situation with Ethan, the flat move, and her new career, before making a final decision. With her parents' move to Oxfordshire, which had almost exactly coincided with her taking up with Ethan three years ago, those cosy chats had become a thing of the past. She was glad to resurrect it here on Christmas Day.

She told her father of her hopes and aspirations for the future, explaining how much she had loved her job and particularly her boss, who was a sweetheart, but how she had felt trapped, that there was nowhere for her to go and that she had been stagnating. She was overjoyed at this new career opportunity and being lucky enough to secure the lease on Rose Cottage brought her a sense of contentment, rightness. She described to her father how that had come about and he remarked how odd it was that life sometimes threw us the answers quite by chance. If she hadn't happened to moan to Jacob about having to move, he would never have thought to mention that Natalie was leaving in a few days and that Rose Cottage would then become vacant.

As soon as Rebecca had set eyes on the picturesque cottage, she had fallen in love with its postcard-like exterior and its homely interior. She could so imagine living there. From the ivy-covered trellises, to the Aga in the lovely country kitchen, to the amazing shower room complete with rainforest shower, all of it was to her liking. She'd literally clapped her hands together in delight when she'd toured the cottage. It didn't get better than this, especially after the dumps she'd visited and the bland new build on which she'd almost signed the lease. When she'd returned to Sugar and Spice, she'd hugged Jacob and Natalie and immediately asked how to get in touch with Mrs Williams, just in case anyone else got in before her. After a brief chat with her new landlady, she'd called the estate agency to cancel the signing of the lease.

Next year was going to be a year that heralded changes for her. Romantic relationships didn't even figure on her agenda, although you could never tell. For now she had enough to keep her occupied and she couldn't wait for the New Year to start.

'I so miss blue cheese,' grumbled Tabitha, patting her stomach, which was replete with her three-course Christmas dinner, mints, crackers and cheddar, and now several Roses she'd snaffled from the tin.

'You've hardly been underfed today,' Jacob pointed out, as he removed the yellow-and-purple wrapper, then popped the caramel into his mouth.

'I'm eating for two, remember?' She grinned.

'That's a fallacy. You're only meant to eat for two in the last two months and only by two hundred calories a day.' Jacob had been checking out all the information. He wanted to be able to help Tabitha properly throughout her pregnancy, plus surely it was part of his duties as godfather?

Tabitha regarded Jacob with tenderness. She was so happy he had blossomed since her revelation about the baby. Always a kind, generous person, Jacob, when faced with the advent of a new family member, had stepped up and not only done his duty, but had become even more involved than Tabitha could ever have hoped. He so much wanted to be a part of her child's life, in many ways he would be a substitute father to it, or at least a father figure, and Tabitha could think of no-one better. All a child needed was love and Jacob had plenty to give.

'I'm going to put some music on. Do you fancy anything in particular?' Jacob asked.

'Normally I'd say something Christmassy, but we've been listening to Christmas songs all week. What about something classical, but soothing?'

'OK, I'm sure I can find something suitable.' Jacob fiddled with his iPod for a bit and then the sound of Chopin filled the air. 'This one's supposed to be suitable for babies.'

Tabitha laughed. Her brother was going to be a nightmare, but in a good way. He wanted everything to be just right for the baby, whereas she was much more laid-back.

'I hadn't planned on playing the baby *The Funeral March* or anything, but I'm sure it could cope with the *1812 Overture*,' she remarked.

Jacob looked doubtful.

As they sat in silence, letting the music wash over them, each lost in their thoughts, Jacob imagined what the future might hold, whilst Tabitha caressed her stomach and told the baby everything would be all right. They would be all right – the three of them. Tabitha became aware of something digging into her back and shuffled around until she could remove it; it was the baby rattle Natalie had given her. How it had got there? She was sure she had put it in her room. She turned it over and over in her hands, examining the craftsmanship. It really did look very old. She said as much to Jacob, who shrugged and returned to listening to the music.

Curiosity getting the better of her, Tabitha turned on her tablet computer and typed a description of the rattle into Google. After much searching she came across one almost exactly like it - she read through the information provided and there was the date manufactured – 1820. It was almost two hundred years old! Surely not. She showed Jacob the page and he agreed that it did look identical to the one Natalie had given her. According to the website only five had ever been made and only one was known to remain, but no-one knew of its whereabouts. Had Natalie given Tabitha an even more precious gift than first thought?

For some reason Jacob went to pick up his snow globe. He still couldn't get over the fact Natalie had managed to get one depicting the street where their bakery was. It was so cool. She must have contacted a specialist supplier. As he picked it up, he noticed the scene had changed. The shops were in darkness, but now a few lights came on in the windows above the shops; the flats overhead.

Must be a trick of the light, thought Jacob, until he saw a door open and a young boy come out, dressed in a thick winter coat. He started walking down the street, past the bakery, and Jacob recognised him as a boy who often came in to buy bread and cakes for his mum. Unsure of how to approach Tabitha with this discovery, Jacob sat mouth agape for a good few minutes, before Tabitha asked him what was up.

Taking the snow globe over to her, Jacob set it down and pointed. Now the young boy was walking back. Had he had been delivering something for his parents, perhaps a belated Christmas card? Tabitha took in the scene, her jaw dropping in a fashion similar to the way Jacob's had. Once the boy had gone indoors, they waited a while, but nothing happened. Jacob picked up the snow globe and shook it. It began to glow. When the snowflakes settled, they both gasped. There was Natalie, sitting by the fire, knitting, in what they presumed was Rose Cottage. Had she actually told them where she was spending Christmas? They tried to think back. No, she'd only said she'd be moving on and Christmas Eve would be her last day at the bakery. She seemed perfectly happy and not remotely upset that she was spending Christmas Day alone. Unexpectedly, Natalie looked up, smiled and then waved at them. Jacob and Tabitha almost fell off their chairs in shock. Had they really just seen what they thought they had? If it wasn't for the fact that Tabitha was pregnant and thus one hundred per cent sober, they would have assumed they had just partaken of too much alcohol.

'Am I going mad, or was that Natalie, and did she just wave at us?' Tabitha asked.

'You're not going mad, either that or we both are, but how is what we saw even possible?' Jacob was stumped. He and Tabitha debated this well into the night, but never solved the mystery.

Natalie stretched and yawned. It had been a busy month,

but she was glad to see her work was up to her usual exacting standards and that everyone was right where they belonged on this important day, even her. She liked to spend Christmas Day seeing how the fruit of her efforts had turned out and she wasn't disappointed this year. She had grown fond of Jacob and so she had been a little naughty and given him the snow globe. He had been partly right in thinking it had been specially commissioned, but not in the way he thought. Likewise, giving Tabitha's baby the rattle she'd kept in case she ever had children of her own, which now she'd passed three hundred years of age, was unlikely to happen, had seemed the right thing to do. Tabitha's child would, as a result, always have Christmas spirit.

Each year Natalie changed her name to something different; call it a quirk, but she felt it necessary to protect her identity. This year it had been Natalie Hope, which she particularly liked as it embodied who she was; Natal – from the Portuguese for Christmas, with Hope, what she tried to create in those she sought to help. In the past she'd been Joy Makepeace, Charity Goodwill and Gabriella Goode, but Natalie Hope felt the most satisfying.

As she cradled her glass of wine, she thought back to some of those she'd helped in the past; Sigmund Freud in Vienna in 1899; Florence Nightingale in 1909; 1920 saw her with Molly Brown, survivor of the *Titanic*; 1937 with the athlete Jesse Owens; 1944 – Winston Churchill, then Prime Minister of Great Britain; 1956 – Sylvia Plath; 1963 – Jackie Kennedy; 1972 – Freddy Mercury; 1981 she spent in Calcutta with Mother Teresa. Although celebrities, each in their own way, they were still people with everyday concerns and Natalie had helped them through some of their darkest moments.

Natalie was glad she had packed earlier today. Since

everything had gone according to plan, she'd be setting off the following morning. Transport had been arranged for her, so she could leave Winstanton unnoticed. She would miss the town and its occupants, but by now she was used to this feeling. She always had to remind herself that her purpose was to create happiness and restore Christmas spirit. Once it was done, it was time to move on.

Even the Christmas Spirit needed a little holiday every so often. She'd packed light: swimsuits, flip-flops, sunhat, suntan lotion. It was hard work restoring peace and goodwill and Natalie had decided Tobago was the perfect antidote to the freezing cold Scottish weather. As she put out the lights and headed for bed, she thought, *Tobago, here I come!*

THE END

Did you get your free short stories yet?

TWO UNPUBLISHED EXCLUSIVE SHORT STORIES.

Interacting with my readers is one of the most fun parts of being a writer. I'll be sending out a monthly newsletter with new release information, competitions, special offers and basically a bit about what I've been up to, writing and otherwise.

You can get the previously unseen short stories, *Mixed Messages* and *Time Is of the Essence*, FREE when you sign up to my mailing list at
www.susanbuchananauthor.com

Did you enjoy *The Christmas Spirit?*

I'd really appreciate if you could leave a review on Amazon. It doesn't need to be much, just a couple of lines. I love reading customer reviews. Seeing what readers think of my books spurs me on to write more. Sometimes I've even written more about characters or created a series because of reader comments. Plus, reviews are SO important to authors. They help raise the profile of the author and make it more likely that the book will be visible on Amazon to more readers. Every author wants their book to be read by more people, and I am no exception! If you're happy to leave a review, please head over to Amazon.

Have you read them all?

The Dating Game

Work, work, work. That's all recruitment consultant Gill does. Her friends fix her up with numerous blind dates, none suitable, until one day Gill decides enough is enough.

Seeing an ad on a bus billboard for Happy Ever After dating agency 'for the busy professional', on impulse she signs up. Soon she has problems juggling her social life as well as her work diary.

Before long she's experiencing laughs, lust and … could it be love? But just when things are looking up for Gill, an unexpected reunion forces her to make an impossible choice.

Will she get her happy ever after, or is she destined to be married to her job forever?

Return of the Christmas Spirit

Susan Buchanan

Christmas is just around the corner when the enigmatic Star begins working at Butterburn library, but not everyone is embracing the spirit of the season.

Arianna is anxious about her mock exams. With her father living abroad and her mother working three jobs to keep them afloat, she doesn't have much support at home.

The bank is threatening to repossess Evan's house, and he has no idea how he will get through Christmas with two children who are used to getting everything they want.

After 23 years of marriage, Patricia's husband announces he's moving out of the family home, and moving in with his secretary. Patricia puts a brave face on things, but inside she's devastated and lost.

Stressed-out Daniel is doing the work of three people in his sales job, plus looking after his kids and his sick wife. Pulled in too many different directions, he hasn't even had a chance to think about Christmas.

Can Star, the library's Good Samaritan, help set them on the path to happiness this Christmas?

Just One Day

'Perfect for fans of *Why Mummy Drinks.*'

Thirty-eight-year-old Louisa has a loving husband, three wonderful kids, a faithful dog, a supportive family and a gorgeous house near Glasgow. What more could she want?

TIME.

Louisa would like, just once, to get to the end of her never-ending to-do list. Whenever she manages to tick something off, another three items pile on.

With Louisa's husband Ronnie working offshore half the month, she is demented trying to cope with everything on her own: the after-school clubs, the homework, the appointments … the constant disasters. And if he dismisses her workload one more time, she may well throttle him.

Juggling running her own wedding stationery business with family life is taking its toll, and the only reason Louisa is still sane is because of her best friends and her sisters.

Fed up with only talking to Ronnie about household bills and the incompetent tradesmen fitting their kitchen, when a handsome stranger pays her some attention on her birthday weekend away, she is flattered, but will she give in to temptation? And will she ever get to the end of her to-do list?

A feel-good, heart-warming story of family and friendship. Ideal for fans of Fiona Gibson.

'This fresh, well-paced story will have you groaning in sympathy as things go from bad to worse.'

~ Book Escapes BabsW67.

Printed in Great Britain
by Amazon

54163981R00118